JELLY
BEAN
SUMMER

JELLY
BEAN
SUMMER

JOYCE MAGNIN

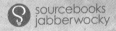

Published by Sourcebooks Jabberwocky, an imprint of Sourcebooks, Inc.
P.O. Box 4410, Naperville, Illinois 60567-4410
(630) 961-3900
Fax: (630) 961-2168
www.sourcebooks.com

Library of Congress Cataloging-in-Publication data is on file with the publisher.

Source of Production: Versa Press, East Peoria, Illinois, USA
Date of Production: March 2017
Run Number: 5008969

Printed and bound in the United States of America.
VP 10 9 8 7 6 5 4 3 2 1

For Elaine

"It's no use going back to yesterday, because I was a different person then."

—Lewis Carroll, *Alice in Wonderland*

One

Westbrook Park, Pennsylvania, 1968

As far as teenage sisters go, my sister Elaine is a doozy. And the thing about doozies is they can be good. They can be bad. Or they can be a combination of good and bad, which is Elaine. On the good side, she helps me with math, and she is an amazing artist—which I will get to in a second. On the bad side, she is boy crazy, listens to what she calls folk music, and, worst of the worst, she has this guinea pig named Jelly Bean that squeals like a banshee every chance she gets. But for some unexplainable reason, Elaine loves Jelly Bean—sometimes I think she loves the guinea pig more than she loves me.

Oh, and Elaine believes in UFOs. She sees them pretty much every night. These sightings have gotten even more frequent since our brother Bud went MIA—missing in action—in Vietnam, a million light years away from us. I have no reason to believe tonight will be any different.

I'm in my bunk—the top bunk—staring at the ceiling, waiting for Elaine to announce her latest sighting. Jeez, you'd think for a teenager she'd have more sense. But Mom says she's ruled more by hormones than brain cells.

"There," she says. "A flying saucer. Quick."

Mom says I should humor her. "It's best, Joyce Anne," she says. She also tells me one day, my hormones will kick in and I'll get all jelly-brained like Elaine. I'm only eleven, and I haven't told Mom, but sometimes, I think my hormones are getting a bit riled up. But that's a discussion for another day.

I wiggle out of my sheets and get to the window even though I am pretty darn sure the alien invaders are all in her head or maybe something our dad calls swamp gas, which sounds gross and smelly.

"Where?" I say with just a little bit of humor.

Elaine lets go of a deep, deep breath and says, "You missed it."

"Of course," I say. "I always do." I give her a glare. "I think you're seeing things."

"I am not seeing things." She folds her arms across her chest and lets out a loud *hummph* noise. But when she does, she bangs into the pig's cage, which is definitely a mistake because she startles Jelly Bean. The rodent squeals and whoops as though space aliens really are invading planet Earth.

"Now look what you did," I say. "You riled the pig, and you know that will rile Dad." I climb into bed and toss my pillow at her because she is still sitting near the window. "Forget about the stupid UFO and go back to bed before we get into trouble."

"You're just a kid," she says. "What do you know?"

Now she's sounding all uppity and tough.

Elaine opens the cage door and lifts Jelly Bean out like she's handling a Fabergé egg. We learned about them in school. They're super-fragile, jewel-encrusted Easter eggs worth millions of dollars. Sheesh. Like Jelly Bean is worth a million bucks.

But I will admit that Jelly Bean is not just an ordinary guinea pig. No, leave it to weird Elaine to have a weird pet. Jelly Bean thinks she's a dog or a very tiny cow. Jelly Bean likes to roam around the front yard and graze on grass and dandelions, and then she waits near the front stoop until someone brings her inside. Like I said, weird.

"Suit yourself," Elaine yell-whispers. "But I know what I saw. I can describe it exactly." She holds her hands apart. "It was about this big." I figure the ship is about the size of a regulation Rawlings football, which of course makes her story even more unbelievable because everyone knows spaceships are huge, definitely bigger than our house. Criminy, didn't she ever see *The Day the Earth Stood Still*? That saucer was bigger than a baseball diamond, and the alien that guarded it was ten stories tall. Still, her descriptions are always pretty good. She once drew a picture of me—well, more like a cartoon—but she got my long legs and blond hair just right. Except in the cartoon, she drew a tail on me. I do not have a tail.

"It's OK," she tells the pig. "It's OK. We believe." Then she looks at me while she cradles the pig like a baby, and it finally stops squealing.

I laugh. "You're a bona fide nutcase."

"I am not. The ship was all silver with a bright band of yellow lights around the middle and had two antennas sticking straight up and…and…"

"And what?" I ask.

"And the antennas had eyes on the ends. Human eyes. One looked that way, while the other looked this way. And then they both looked straight at me."

"Of course they had eyes," I say. "Everything does."

Elaine has a thing about eyes. She sees them everywhere. In the clouds. In tree bark. In ripples in a stream. And to tell the truth, her own eyes are pretty magnificent. Elaine could spot a four-leaf clover in a nine-acre field if we were driving in the car going sixty miles an hour. I would never say this to her face, but I think it's her weird-sightedness that makes her such a good artist.

She's so good that if she draws an apple, you might try to pick it right up off the page and take a bite. She doesn't draw apples all that much though. Now she's more into painting psychedelic flowers everywhere—even on her face. Elaine claims to be a flower child, which means she wears hip-hugger jeans, gauzy blouses, flashes the peace sign whenever she can, and, like I said, she draws flowers on everything. She even painted a bright-yellow daisy with a peace symbol as the center on my father's lunch box. He was not too thrilled.

Elaine said it would make him smile—which is something Dad doesn't do much these days. Not since Bud went missing.

"The antennas did have eyes!" Elaine insists. "I saw them!" She puts Jelly Bean back in her cage, checks the latch twice, and climbs into bed. "You never believe me. No one does. Ever."

Thinking she is going to burst into tears, I roll onto my side and look over the edge of my bunk. "OK, did it make a noise?"

"It made a low *bzzzzzzzzzzzzzz*."

"Maybe it was a hummingbird. The rare Pennsylvania silver-and-yellow-streaked vampire hummingbird. They only fly at night. It wanted to suck your blood." I say the last part with a Dracula accent.

Elaine kicks the bottom of my mattress. "Shut up. Hummingbirds don't come out at night. And there is no such thing as a vampire hummingbird."

"Think that if you want, but I'd wear turtlenecks from now on."

"Creep!" she hollers.

"Pig nose!" I holler right back.

That's when the door flies open. It's Dad.

"Now you did it." I try to hit her with my pillow.

Dad steps into the room. "I'm hearing a lot of squealing and arguing."

"It's her fault," Elaine says. "She called me a nutcase because I saw another spaceship."

I swear that even in the darkened room, I can see my father's eyeballs roll around like googly eyes on a sock puppet. "There are no alien invaders," he says. He must have missed Mom's lecture on how we need to humor Elaine. "Now go to sleep. Both of you."

Dad closes the door, and the instant I hear the click, Elaine says, "I did see it. No one believes me."

Jelly Bean grunts, and I hear small whoops like she's gearing up to squeal like a banshee again.

"Keep your stupid pig quiet," I say.

Elaine kicks my bunk. "If you don't like it, why don't you just move out?"

"Maybe I will."

If I had a place to go, that is.

I stare up at the ceiling and the weird shadows that always dance around at night, shadows from the streetlight outside and from the hall light that seeps under the bedroom door like a stream. The weird, scraggly shadows are the branches of the peach tree outside our window. But even though I know that, they're still a little scary. I'm never sure if Elaine sees them or not, so I never say anything.

She kicks at my bunk. "Someday you'll see. Someday you'll believe."

I close my eyes, trying to think about the things I do believe in. Things I believe even though I can't prove them. Like Elaine believes in her UFOs. But I can't think of anything except maybe electricity, so I lean over the side rail and say, "I believe you. I believe you see the flying saucers."

"That's not the same," Elaine says.

So that night, while the house is quiet and the shadows dance, I think about believing. I stare at the ceiling and think about the night and the moon and the stars. I think about believing, and I think about seeing. Then the ceiling makes me think about the roof and how I can see the stars and the world so clearly when I'm up there. Bud and I used to go up and sit on the wide, flat roof and look at the stars sometimes. He taught me about the constellations. I think about them for a minute, and I think about Bud until I feel a tear form in my left eye. I swipe it away, and that's when it hits me with all the gravitational pull the moon can muster.

The roof.

I will move to the roof.

Two

At breakfast, I sit at the kitchen table and work on three things:

1. A bowl of Rice Krispies with a sliced banana on top
2. How exactly to tell Mom the big decision I made last night
3. My courage

My mother is at the sink washing a large, blue mixing bowl. She's not talking. Just humming a low tune like she always does when she washes dishes or sews hems or picks aphids off her African violet plants. The tune seems to take her miles away.

I'm not sure how my mother will react when I tell her I want to move to the roof, even though I've been up there a thousand times. It's…peaceful, quiet. The roof is flat like our patio. I've already set up a beach chair. I can sit up there, far from everything, and just be quiet. But not in the same way our house is quiet. I think the quiet inside a house when one of the family is missing is so sad, you can feel it with every breath you take. It even has a taste. To me, the quiet tastes like butterscotch. I know butterscotch isn't supposed to be a bad taste, but that's just it. Everything that's supposed to be good isn't anymore.

Maybe on the roof, things will be better.

Fortunately, I don't have to deal with Dad right away. He's already gone to work. Dad's a plumber and always leaves early in the summer. "Want to beat the heat," he says. Then he always tells Mom, "Find me if you hear anything." Then Mom pats Dad's cheek and says, "I will. I'll send the mayor if I have too."

She always sends him off with a cooler of iced tea and two extra shirts because he sweats like a pig. Although I never saw a pig sweat. Not even oh-so-precious Jelly Bean.

Elaine is sitting across from me, staring into her bowl of cereal. Probably trying to see what kind of pictures the Krispies make as she swirls the milk with her spoon. More eyeballs, I figure.

Polly, our big, brown dog, sits under the table waiting for handouts. I slip her the piece of bacon Dad left on his plate. Finally, while Polly licks my hand, I muster up my courage and just blurt it out like I am a balloon and someone popped me with a pin and all the air whooshed out.

"I'm moving to the roof today."

My mother stops humming. She snorts air out of her nose. Elaine laughs like a hyena.

"Now why in the world would you want to move to the roof?" Mom asks.

"Because I...just want to."

"Fine with me," Elaine says. "I'll get the room all to myself."

"And besides," I say. "She keeps seeing flying saucers, and Jelly Bean squeals all the time, and...and everything around here is too damn sad." I drop my spoon in the bowl. The milk splashes.

"Joyce Anne," Mom says. "We don't talk like that."

"Well, it is," I say. "Ever since Bud went MI..."

"A," Elaine says. "You don't know anything."

"I know it's A." I glare at her. "I had to swallow before I could say it. And it is sad here. Ever since the news came, everyone is so mopey. Dad sits in front of the TV watching war news, or he hangs out in his garage building things he never talks about."

I push my bowl away and look at Mom, who's still looking at me like she's trying to vaporize my head with her eyes. "And I hear you crying sometimes," I tell her. "I know you don't mean for me to hear. But I do."

Mom closes her eyes for just a second, and then she looks away toward her violets.

"And I'm sick of Elaine calling me a creep, and, well, I just want to live on the roof. I can do it. I'll bring my sleeping bag, my books, my binoculars, and whatever else I need."

"What if it rains?" Elaine asks. And she mouths the word *creep* at me while Mom isn't looking.

I mouth *pig nose* back at her. "I have the big beach umbrella, and I'll set up my tent. And if it rains too hard, I'll come inside. Sheesh, I'm not stupid."

"Why don't you pitch the tent in the backyard?" Mom asks.

"Because I…I like the roof. It's quiet. I can see the stars."

Mom lets go of a huge sigh. She looks at Elaine. "You *have* been seeing a lot of flying saucers and—"

Elaine stands up. Her milk sloshes. "You don't believe me either. No one does."

Mom doesn't say anything about believing or not believing. She just tells Elaine to sit down and "finish your breakfast and drink all that orange juice. It's too expensive to waste."

Then she looks at me. "You sure about this?"

I nod.

Mom goes back to the sink. She rinses a bowl and sets it in the drainer. Then she turns back and says, "Fine, Joyce. If you want to spend the summer on the hot roof, go ahead. Just don't fall off."

"I won't. I've been up there plenty of times."

"And don't take the dog," Mom says. "Remember what happened the last time you tried that stunt."

I do remember. I made a canvas sling out of an old tent and tried to hoist Polly up to the roof. She was not happy, and I didn't get her very far off the ground before Mom caught me. She unhitched Polly and grounded me for the rest of the week.

I look straight at Elaine. "Maybe I'll just bring Jelly Bean."

Elaine smacks the table. "You will not. Don't you dare touch her."

Mom pats my shoulder. "But I am not bringing your meals up there."

"You can put them in the basket, and I'll hoist them up," I say.

I already have a basket system in place for times when I go up to search for balls, Wiffle bats, and even Barbie dolls. Once, I lowered a baby bird with a broken wing down. It died an hour later. Mom said I rescued it too late.

The other day, I hoisted up the beach chair and the beach umbrella. Made myself a pretty nice sitting spot where I can see the whole neighborhood—maybe even the whole world—clear down the street into our playground, called Scullion Field. I can see everyone's backyards and driveways. I can see past the chain-link fence that separates the playground from the woods. And then there's nothing but sky.

Mom shakes her head. "I will not put your meals in a basket. You'll eat with the family."

I let go of a breath. "Oh, all right, I'll come down for meals."

"And to use the bathroom, I hope," Elaine says. "Don't want you stinking up all the air up there."

I stick my tongue out at her.

"Just please, Joyce Anne, be careful," Mom says. She goes back to her dirty dishes. And her humming.

"You mean I get the room all to myself?" Elaine says. "For real?"

"Guess so." Mom hums a little.

"Cool." Elaine raises her eyebrows at me as though she's just been given the keys to where they keep the Fabergé eggs.

"Now you can invite your little UFO friends inside for a tea party." I slip Polly another piece of bacon. "If Martians drink tea."

"Probably green tea," Mom says.

I laugh. "Good one, Mom. Green tea for little green men."

"Creep."

"Pig nose."

∞

So that day, I make the big move. I pack a bunch of snacks I figure won't go bad in the sun. Mom gives me a thermos of iced tea and pats my cheek. "Be careful," she says.

My friend Linda Costello helps me get my stuff up there. I don't think she's too keen on the idea of climbing onto the roof. So she stays on the ground and loads my basket while I hoist it. I don't have that much. A sleeping bag, a basket of books, my all-important World War II surplus binoculars, and, of course, the tent.

Linda doesn't stick around long after we're done because she has to go shoe shopping with her mom. After the last basket is up, I climb down to say good-bye.

Linda jumps on her bike. "Are you sure about this?" she asks, sounding just like Mom.

"Yeah, why not?" I say.

"I think you're crazy."

"No I'm not. It's kind of like having my own room."

Linda shakes her head. "I gotta go before my mom starts hollering for me. She hates it when she has to holler."

Polly is sitting on her haunches near the ladder. I pat her head and then hug her neck. She looks a little sad. "Don't worry, girl. I'll be up and down all the time, and we'll still go for runs and to the woods and stuff."

The ladder is tilted against the wall next to our peach tree, and I have to push one of the smaller branches away.

Mom planted the tree when I was five. Dad thought she was

squirrelly for keeping a peach pit resting on a paper towel on the kitchen windowsill for weeks. She kept it between two potted African violets as though that particular spot held some secret meaning, some magnetic pull that would make the seed have special growing powers. It's possible she even said those very words.

My mother had been growing African violets ever since I can remember. She cares for them like each bloom is a Fabergé egg.

And that's where she put the peach pit. Right under the African violet leaves. No one dared move it because Mom had something up her sleeve, some use for this now dried-out seed that might or might not possess magical powers.

One cold, cold February day, just after a snowfall, my mother took the seed out to the side yard. Elaine was at school. Polly and I watched Mom brush a small patch of snow away, exposing the hard, brown soil, and dig a small hole, not very deep, with a silver tablespoon. She placed the peach pit in the hole and covered it with dirt. She didn't pack it down or water it. She put a little snow on top of the small mound, and then she set a large, glass peanut butter jar on top just as the sun broke through gray clouds.

"There," she said, brushing her hands together. "In time, we will have peaches." It was like an incantation.

And her prediction came true. Here it is, six years later, and the tips of the top branches reach the top windowsill of our house.

As I climb the ladder, I can see the tree perfectly. It sure grew fast—tall and wide. By August, it will be heavy with peaches—the best peaches. The peaches Dad and I use to make homemade peach ice cream. Ice cream that Dad calls "an experience."

Elaine sticks her head out our bedroom window and says, "Have fun, creep." A small gust of wind blows her brown hair across her face.

"Oh, don't you worry," I say. "I'll have fun and—" I gasp and point toward the backyard. "What's that? Tiny, little people climbing out of a tiny spaceship? You better go greet them."

"I hope you fall off." She pulls the window closed.

"Space creatures." I shake my head and step onto the roof and survey my tidy little camp in the middle of a black tar sea. It is a tiny island in a big universe.

Three

Row houses are all the same. Boring, redbrick houses lined up one after the other, like Monopoly houses. Each one has the same three bedrooms and one bathroom. The houses are attached in neat rows of twelve with a wide, grassy break or a street between each row. Pretty boring.

The houses are linked by flat roofs covered with layers of sin-black tar. All the roofs have TV antennas on them. Who knows? Maybe the dishes call the aliens Elaine sees. Ha! Now that's a weird thought.

The houses that are sandwiched between the ends have a skylight in the bathroom operated by chains to allow light and air to come in. We live in an end house, which means we have a window in our bathroom, and we have an extra side yard. I think having a bathroom window and a side yard makes our house captain of the row—or at least our half of the row.

I stand near the beach umbrella and survey my camp, which

isn't much. There's the wooden beach chair, which has a tan canvas back and a ratty, old canvas cushion that is kind of lumpy, like mice are living inside. The umbrella is also canvas but has turned the most disgusting shade of yellow and has stains that no one can identify. A red Wawa Dairy milk crate holds books and comic books, a deck of cards, my diary, and my binoculars.

My small cooler is stuffed with Tastykakes—especially Jelly Krimpets—brownies, Herr's potato chips, and the thermos of iced tea Mom made. All in all, not bad for my first day of roof living, except it *is* really hot. I feel the heat from the tar through my sneakers, but the shade from the umbrella makes it bearable.

I use my binoculars to scope out the wider universe. I look as far as I can, across our alley and into the Wilburs' backyard to their bomb shelter, a big, ugly gray building made from cinder blocks. Everyone believes it is lined with lead and stocked chockful with canned ham, baked beans, and toilet paper. The Wilburs built it a few years earlier when everyone was afraid the commies were all riled up and ready to drop the A-bomb on us. I asked my brother once what we should do if the commies did haul off and drop the bomb.

"Just kiss your ass good-bye," he said.

I spy down Palmer Mill Drive and over Scullion Field, where the baseball diamond is sprinkled with kids in shorts and caps. Most of the caps are red. That's because Westbrook Park Elementary's school colors are red and white. I can hear the players' voices on the slight breeze. I look farther into the woods that begin just where Scullion Field ends, separated by a tall chain-link fence that keeps the occasional foul ball from flying into the trees.

A robin is perched in an evergreen, and an orange cat slinks along the green bleachers at the park. Flowers burst into view, yellow with black centers, wild black-eyed Susans poking their faces through the fence.

I see eight or nine round, plastic swimming pools—all in a row behind the houses. I see people moving about from house to car, garage to house. Mrs. Fulmer is lugging grocery bags while her spoiled son, Clarence, watches from the door. Sheesh. There goes Joey Patrillo on his bike. Denna DeLuca is sitting on a beach chair in her front yard catching some sun. Then I hear a garage door slam shut.

Row-house garages are part of the house—they're neatly tucked underneath. The large doors have a sound I'd recognize anywhere. They make a rattling *whoosh-bang* sound when they go up and a rattling *whoosh-bang-click* sound when they go down. Sometimes, they jump their track and derail like a train.

You can get into the garage through the basement. Dad uses our garage to store his plumber tools and stuff. He has a large band saw he uses to cut wood. It is also where he hangs his fishing rods and keeps his waders in neat rows like soldiers. Some people actually park their cars inside the garage, but my father parks his work truck in our short driveway and the car out front on the street. He always looks for a spot not too far from the house and gets angry when someone else parks right in front. Mom doesn't care so much if she parks up the street or down. Unless she has groceries.

They never park in the garage because Dad thinks that is unsafe.

"Carbon monoxide," he says. "Carbon monoxide."

After he first said that, I had an image of our whole family waking up dead one morning due to a buildup of the deadly gas. But now I think he only says it so he can keep the garage all to himself. Lately, Dad has been holed up in the garage after watching the evening news. He won't tell anyone what he is doing in there, and he keeps the doors locked during the day. He hung two big *Keep out!* signs: one on the outside garage door and one on the door that opens to the basement.

Still looking through the glasses—that's Dad's word for binoculars—I find the garage door I heard. Nothing interesting. Just Mr. DePalma pulling out his lawnmower. I turn south and peer over more and more rooftops until I see something that nearly knocks me off my feet. In fact, I stumble backward a little because I can't believe my eyes. It's another set of binoculars looking at me!

My first thought is that I should drop my pair and run. But I take a breath and focus in for a tighter view. It's a boy. A boy wearing a green shirt—the kind my Dad wears to work—and blue jeans with rolled-up cuffs. The pants look two sizes too big. He has hardly any hair. A buzz cut like they gave Bud when he first joined the army. The boy just stands there looking through his lenses, looking at me looking at him.

I think about waving, but I'm not sure if I should wave to a stranger. He looks a little older than me, and for a second, I consider the possibility that he is one of the lunatics my dad is always telling Elaine and me to be on the lookout for. He definitely does not go to Westbrook Park Elementary School. I would have seen him.

The boy stays peeled on me in kind of a Mexican-binocular-roof standoff. And then, slowly, he raises his hand with his palm facing me and waves but just at the wrist. My heart speeds as I hold the lenses in my right hand and raise my left. Palm out, I slowly, cautiously wave back. I'm still not sure I should wave, but I do because I don't want him to think I am rude. Or a spy.

I calculate he is standing on a roof of a house about midway down Crestwood Drive.

He lowers his hand. I lower mine. And then he lets his binoculars drop like something scared him. They bounce against his chest once, and then he is gone.

For a second, I wonder if I really saw him. Maybe he is an alien from one of Elaine's flying saucers. Or maybe he is a ghost. But, nah, not in broad daylight. No, it was a boy—absolutely for sure. A boy with binoculars who now knows I am here on the roof.

I go back to watching the neighborhood. I look toward the second row on our street. Mrs. Duthart is in her side yard raking under her overgrown azalea bushes. Her fat, little beagle, Peaches, is running around barking to beat the band.

Mrs. Duthart lives in the house on the other side of the break. Our side yards butt against each other but are separated by a chain-link fence. From up on the roof, I can see there are lots of fences in Westbrook Park. Dad says that good fences make for good neighbors. Mrs. Duthart doesn't get that. She hates my guts. I don't know why. She pretty much hates everybody's guts. David Hazel calls her Mrs. Du*fart* and laughs like mad every time he says it, like he is Red Skelton.

The Hazels live in the house attached to ours. David Hazel's claim to neighborhood fame is that he got hit by a car and broke his leg. It was a pretty big deal for a while because nothing like that usually happens in Westbrook Park. But it did for him. He got all kinds of neat gifts and comic books. My mother even baked him a batch of cookies. It was like he got famous for getting clobbered by a Buick.

Elaine and I went to visit him a couple of times and even helped him scratch inside the big, white cast with a coat hanger we stretched out. Mrs. Hazel caught us and yelled.

"You'll give him an infection!" she squawked like a big, fat chicken. Mrs. Hazel hates my guts too.

I look back, hoping my mysterious Binocular Boy is there again. He isn't. So I drop the glasses to my chest and sit in the beach chair. This is the life. No Elaine, no Jelly Bean, no sad Dad or Mom, just me on top of the world. Me and the moon and the stars that will come out soon.

After a while, I hear Polly barking. She is in the front yard sitting on one of the brown spots where grass refuses to grow. There are lots of spots like that on our lawn. Lots of smallish brown spots with tufts of grass or weeds growing out of them. From up here, they look like a congregation of balding heads.

Polly has different barks for different situations. This one is her Dad's-home bark. Polly can hear Dad's truck with her super-duper dog ears when it is two blocks away.

Dad is coming down the street—home from work. This is good and bad. Good because I am hungry as a bear fresh from hibernation. Mom usually makes meat loaf on Wednesday, and I could eat half the loaf and ten pounds of mashed potatoes today. My mom makes the best mashed potatoes and meat loaf on the planet.

But Dad coming home is also bad because he doesn't know I moved to the roof. So instead of dashing down for supper, I figure it might be a good idea to wait. Maybe Mom will tell him about me being on the roof, and he'll get all his yelling done before I show my face. I'm pretty sure he will yell. So I wait, hoping Mom will give him the news and work some of her Mom magic on him. While I wait, I look through the glasses again, and sure enough, Binocular Boy is back. My heart speeds as I wave. He waves back and holds up a large piece of cardboard: *My name is Brian.*

Brian. Wow. I look around, but I don't see anything to write my name on except my diary. I tear out a page, find my pen, and write *Joyce* as big as I can on the small piece of blue-lined paper. I hold it up.

He zeros in on the page. He drops his glasses and like ten seconds later holds up another sign: *Hi, Joyce.*

My heart pounds. It is possible I am getting myself into trouble, but the allure of the whole thing is too hard to ignore. *Allure.* It is one of my new favorite words. I got it from Elaine's *Vogue* I was reading a few days ago.

I turn my page over and write: *Hi, Brian.*

I hold it up and wait, but he doesn't make another sign. Instead, I just see him smile.

My heart beats so hard, I think I might get sick, so I drop my binoculars into the milk crate and scoot down the ladder.

∞

When I walk into the house, I am hoping for three things:

1. Dad isn't angry I am living on the roof.
2. Elaine isn't blabbing to him about it and telling him how I don't believe in her space creatures and how I complain about Jelly Bean.
3. Mom put plenty of butter on the mashed potatoes.

I head straight to the steps and listen. Dad is in the shower, and I am glad for that. Next, I head to the kitchen. Elaine is setting the table.

"Hey, creep," she says. "How 'bout helping?"

"Not my turn," I say. I hate that she calls me *creep* so much. Mom says to ignore it. Which isn't always easy.

"Did you tell him, Mom?"

Mom looks at me. "Tell him what?"

"You know. About me moving to the roof."

"Not yet, dear." She goes back to the stove.

I start to take my seat at the table, but Mom stops me. The eyes in the back of her head see me. "What do you think you're doing, little girl? You get washed up first."

"Oh, sorry," I say and head for the kitchen sink.

"Not there. Upstairs. And use soap."

"Dad's taking his shower."

"So wait," Elaine says. "Sheesh, you're such a dummy."

I look at my mother, hoping she will say something to Elaine about calling me names. But she doesn't. As usual. Well, as usual since Bud went missing. It's like adding any more upset-ness into the air could ignite the whole house on fire, so Mom just ignores things. "Just wait until he's done. In the meantime, go sit in the living room with those filthy hands."

I hold my hands up. They are pretty filthy.

I hear a door close upstairs, so I run up to get washed. Which I do quickly and run back downstairs. Just as I'm showing Mom my hands, Dad comes to the table. He is a big man with broad shoulders and large hands. He has a wide smile that shows off his missing left incisor. He has bright-blue eyes and is going bald on the top of his head.

The table is set with the food in bowls of different colors and sizes, including one large green bowl that holds my favorite:

mashed potatoes. Elaine and I sit across from each other, which makes it easy for me to kick her and flick the occasional pea in her direction. Polly sneaks under the table. Dad always shoos her into the living room, or at least he tries to. She always sneaks back.

Dad still doesn't know about me moving to the roof, and it's hard to keep my monkey nerves under control. My legs keep bouncing. Maybe Mom will wait until after supper to tell him. Some news goes best on a full stomach.

'Course that hadn't helped much the night we got the news about Bud. We were just finishing up our fruit dessert, sliced pears, when the doorbell rang.

I answered it. Two army officers were standing there with grim faces. They each removed their hats and held them tucked in their armpits when I opened the door. The soldier on the left held a small, yellowish envelope.

"Is your mother or father at home?" he asked.

But I didn't answer because Dad was standing behind me in a flash. Like he sensed something. He snatched the envelope from the soldier, who tried to speak but didn't get the chance because Dad pulled the door closed. A lump formed in my stomach because I had the sneaking suspicion that we were about to get some pretty bad news.

Dad read the telegram aloud. It informed us that Private

First Class Arthur Robert Magnin had been reported missing somewhere in Hanoi. My father's brow crinkled like an autumn leaf. My mother stood there. Staring. Elaine didn't say a word. Neither did I. Not for a whole minute or two until I blurted out, "What do they mean missing? How can he be missing?"

Dad pushed the telegram into Mom's hand.

"It could mean many things," Mom said with a shaky voice. "So we'll just hope and pray that Bud will come home safe and sound very soon."

And that was all she said.

Dad patted my head. He smiled at Elaine and then walked upstairs. I heard his bedroom door close. Mom went up after him. Elaine just sat on the couch with Polly.

I ran outside, feeling like the house was too small and hot. The peach tree was in full bloom. Tiny, green peaches were forming under the flowers and pushing the blossoms to the ground. While I stood there not knowing what to do, one of the buds tumbled to the ground.

My news—the news about me moving up to the roof—isn't going to make Dad sad the way the news about Bud made him. But I still wanted Mom to wait until after supper to tell him his youngest daughter has moved to the roof.

I look around the table. *Yep. No smiles.*

Mom still hasn't told Dad about me moving to the roof. I figure she's waiting until after he's had his fill of meat loaf.

Saying grace before a meal—well, supper mostly—is a ritual we never forget. I don't think I could eat supper if it hadn't first been prayed over. It's the same prayer every night. I figure God is pretty sick of it—if God gets sick of things.

It was Elaine's turn.

"ThankyouLordforfoodwetaketodousgoodforJesus'ssakeamen."

Grace has become one long word.

We all dig into the bowls and pass them around. Peas, mashed potatoes, applesauce. Dad divvies up the meat loaf as usual.

"Had a funny thing happen at work today," he says.

Good. When Dad tells stories about work, it means he's in a good mood.

"And what's that?" Mom asks as she scoops peas from the serving bowl and plops them on her plate.

Dad is munching meat loaf. "I found something in Mrs. Watson's toilet."

"Ewwwwww, Daaaaaaaad," Elaine says. "We're eating."

He smiles. "No, no, wait until I tell you. She called me because her lavatory was clogged."

Dad often uses fancy plumbing vocabulary—*lavatory* is fancy for toilet. I swallow my mashed potatoes and turn a listening

31

ear because I, for one, want to know what was clogging Mrs. Watson's plumbing.

"Had to take the whole thing apart," Dad says. "Snaked it out good, and then…" He sets his knife and fork on his plate and raises his arms and says with a clap, "Up it came."

"What, Dad?" I ask. "What came up?"

I glance at Elaine. She looks like whatever was clogging Mrs. Watson's toilet is now clogging her throat.

"A trout," Dad says. "I figured it for about a pound and a half. This big." He holds his hands about six inches or so apart. About half the size of Elaine's flying saucer.

I laugh. "That's impossible. How can a fish get caught in a toilet?"

Dad picks up his utensils and goes back to work on his meat loaf. He shakes his knife in my direction. "I figure it got into the sewer line and swam into Mrs. Watson's john. It was too big to make it into the bowl, but here's the really strange part—"

"Oh, Art, there's more?" Mom mixes three peas into her forkful of potatoes.

"It was still alive," he says.

"Oh no," Mom says. "What did you do?"

"Gross," Elaine says. "Dad, stop talking about it."

Dad looks at Mom and then at me. "What could I do?" he

says. "I cracked it on the head with my hammer and tossed it in the trash. I wasn't about to bring it home for supper."

That's when Elaine loses it. She starts to cry, drops her fork, and dashes away from the table, sobbing, "That poor fish. That poor, poor fish. Father, how could you?"

I hold back a laugh.

"Art," Mom says. "You know how sensitive Elaine is. Things like that will give her nightmares."

Dad poked at his food. "Oh, I'm sorry. I didn't mean to upset her. I'll talk to her later."

Sheesh. Elaine really is sensitive and gets upset easily. I think it has to do with her being an artist. But seriously, what else was he supposed to do with the fish?

With Elaine gone from the table, Mom must think it's a good time to tell Dad about my roof thing. She pulls her fork from her lips and rests it on the side of her dish. "Joyce Anne has decided to move onto the roof for a little while."

I swallow. Hard. I cringe and close my eyes, waiting for Dad to blast me from one end of the house to the other, like I was shot from a cannon. Silence. I open my left eye and look at him, trying to see if his face is getting red. I open the other eye. That's when he hollers.

"She *what*? She can't live on the roof. It's dangerous. It's dirty."

"But, Dad," I say. "It's not that dirty, and it's not even that dangerous. I've been up there lots of times. You taught me how, remember?"

"She's got a point," Mom says.

"I don't care. That's no place for a girl to sleep. What if she wakes up and walks right off the roof? What then, little girl? You'll break both legs and probably your neck. I forbid it." Then he slams the table with his big, meaty fist, stands up, and finishes hollering.

"The roof is no place for a girl. Not at night. It's one thing if you go up there to fetch a ball or something, but you will not sleep there. And what will you do if the tar men come, huh? What then?"

"But, Dad, I'm sick of Elaine and her stupid UFOs. I hate her stupid pig that squeals all the time. I can't stand her, and besides, I already moved my stuff up there, and I won't fall off. I'm not a dummy like Elaine says I am." I take a huge breath. "I made my camp in the middle, so even if I do wake up and start walking, I'll wake up. It's not that easy to fall off the damn roof with that edge around it." I cover my mouth with my hand. I have never, ever said a cuss word to Dad before. But he doesn't even flinch.

"We don't say *damn*," Mom says.

"Well, I just did." I look straight at Dad.

"And I didn't think of the tar men," Mom says. "If they come around, you'll have to move back to your room."

I hadn't thought of them either. Tar men have a way of just showing up with their stinking, black cauldrons of boiling tar, which they spread on the roofs to keep them from leaking. But I refuse to let that stop me.

"I'll move down if they come and then move back up once the tar is cooled and dry."

Dad is fuming like one of the tar men's cauldrons. But I figure sometimes Dad likes to fume—not so much about what is happening at the moment but because underneath, he's fuming about other things—like a crotchety old customer who gave him a rubber check. Or, worse, like his only son is missing.

He is really mad at the world, not me. I figure this day is one of those days, even though for at least a couple of minutes when he was telling us about Mrs. Watson's toilet trout, he seemed in a better mood. Maybe that's why Mom thought he might not go berserk. Boy, was she wrong. Steam is coming out of his ears and his nostrils. He takes a deep breath and nearly sucks all the air out of the kitchen.

"Now, Art," Mom says. "What harm can it do? She won't fall off. And if the tar men come, we'll get her down in time."

Dad sits back down and picks up his fork. He stabs a piece

of meat loaf and then another and then another, and I have to wonder who he is really stabbing. "Fine. Have it your way. She falls off and breaks her neck, it ain't my fault." Then he looks at me. "And don't go near anyone's antennas or skylights."

"Thank you, Daddy," I say before he can say anything else. I jump up, kiss his cheek, and dash straight to my room. Well, my old room. The one Elaine has already entirely taken over. I need a couple more books, and I am planning on swiping her flashlight in case the batteries in mine die and I need to see in the dark.

Jelly Bean squeals the instant I close the door. She always sounds like someone is sticking her with pins. Elaine is sitting on her bed with her music blaring. She is drawing in her big sketchbook with her fancy pencils.

"Hey," I say.

"I can't believe Dad," she says without looking up from her book. "That poor fish."

"It was funny. A fish in the toilet." I move closer. "Whatcha drawing?"

She shrugs.

"Little green men with big bug eyes and pear-shaped heads?"

"None of your business. Why are you here anyway? Did Dad put the kibosh on the roof? I heard him hollering at you."

"Mom straightened him out."

"So how come you're not up there then?"

"I need a couple of things."

"Well, get them and get out." She goes back to her drawing. I try to sneak a peek, but she keeps it hidden. And that's when I remember Brian and the way he was writing signs to me. Elaine's sketchbook would be really handy for signs. I could write nice, big messages. She keeps an extra one under her bed, but how can I sneak it out of the room without telling her about Brian? All I need is for her to find out about him. She'd tell Mom, who'd tell Dad, and then Dad would go all berserk again, and he wouldn't calm down. He'd probably climb onto the roof and throw all my stuff down and forbid me from ever, ever going on the roof again.

I open the closet. Elaine keeps her camp flashlight in there, but it's probably buried under the pile of dirty clothes crammed inside.

"Hey," Elaine says. "What are you doing?"

"I need a flashlight."

"You got your own."

"Aw, come on," I say. "Let me take yours too. Just for backup."

Jelly Bean squeals even louder. Elaine opens her cage, which is right next to her bed, and lifts her out. She hugs the rodent to her chest and strokes her head. "Shhh, it's OK. The creep will be gone soon." Jelly Bean wiggles around until her little white-and-brown body is snuggled under Elaine's chin.

"So," I say. "Can I take it?"

"Yeah, just don't break it."

I dig through the mound of smelly clothes and locate the flashlight. I test it. It shines bright. I click it off. But I still need the sketchbook. There is no way in jumpin' blue heck she will give me her spare. Sketchbooks are like sacred or something to Elaine. She has stacks of them filled with drawings and paintings and little doodles and scribbles. She loves flowers and birds and mountains and cows and spaceships and, of course, eyeballs. Lots and lots of eyes. They're creepy.

I need to get her out of the room. I lean against my dresser, considering the situation. A diversion is needed. If I were a spy, I'd have a smoke bomb. But as luck would have it, I don't have to do anything because the phone rings downstairs. *Please let it be for Elaine. Please.* I cross my fingers and wait, and then a few seconds later, Mom calls. "Elaine, it's for you."

"The phone," I say. "Mom just said it's for you."

"I heard her," Elaine says as she gently sets Jelly Bean in her cage.

I wait a little bit until I'm sure she's gone. Then I slide under the bunk like Mickey Mantle sliding into second and snatch the sketchbook. Perfect.

It's too risky to carry it downstairs and outside, so I open the window screen and toss it out into the side yard. Then I dash down the steps with my pillow, the flashlight, and a copy of *The Field Guide to the Stars and Planets* crammed inside the pillowcase. "See ya," I say.

Dad is in his chair watching the news. I pause for just a second and watch the TV. They're talking about the war. I hate the news. All of it.

I swallow and look back at my father. I figure he's missing Bud. The other day, Dad and I were driving down Baltimore Pike, and he had to pull over and cry a little after hearing an old song on the radio. It was some old-timey song—"Old Danny Boy" or "Oh, Danny Boy." He pretended he wasn't crying. Said he had to check to see if the trunk was shut. But I saw him back there wiping his eyes.

"See ya," I say again.

Dad doesn't say anything. I think it's because he is holding his breath.

I miss Bud too. I'm worried about him too, but I never say it out loud. I guess I don't want Dad to worry that I'm missing Bud at the same time he's missing him. Sometimes, it's possible to have too much worry under one roof.

Four

From my perch on the roof, I have a clear view of the sky, steel blue on the fringes but bright and blue like a robin's egg for the most part. There isn't a cloud to be seen, and that's a good thing because I don't want it to rain. Not on my first night under the stars on top of the world. With plenty of daylight still to go, I sit on the beach chair and peer through my binoculars, hoping to see Brian. Now that I am armed with Elaine's sketchbook, I can write larger messages. I scan the horizon and then bring the glasses around in time to see Linda riding down the sidewalk on her bike. I watch until she rides onto my lawn and I can't see her anymore. I jump up and dash to the edge of the roof. "Linda, come on up."

"You come down."

"No. Come on up. It's great."

I know Linda is scared, but she has to at least try. "Come on. You'll be OK."

"The peach tree is in the way," she calls.

"Just get on the other side. No big deal."

Then I hear her holler, "Owwww."

I look over the edge. "What's wrong?"

"Stupid tree poked me in the butt."

I laugh. "Don't take it personal. Just climb up the ladder."

She makes her way up, shaky at first, but she makes it. I help her off the wooden ladder and over the roof edge. I will admit that even for me, that part of the climb is scary. I have to take a deep breath every time.

"Hey," I say.

Linda looks mighty nervous. Her legs are shaking.

"It's OK," I say.

"I've never been on the roof before."

I take her hand. "Come on. Closer to my camp."

"Whatcha doin'?" she asks. I think she's trying to keep her cool.

"You can have my chair."

"Nah, I'll stand." She still sounds pretty scared. "I just came to ask if you wanted to go down to the playground."

"No, not now. I'd rather sit up here." I glance toward Brian's roof. Could Linda be trusted with such top-secret information?

"How come? You ain't doin' nothin' but sittin' up here."

"I know, but…"

"But what?" Linda smiles and smashes her glasses into her face.

"Can you keep a secret?" I whisper.

"Sure. What gives?"

I spill the beans—every single one. I tell her about Brian and the signs and how I am waiting on the roof for him to come back.

"No kidding? You're brave. How do you know he's not a nut or an ax murderer or somethin'?" Linda pushes her hand through her curly hair and untangles a knot.

"I just know," I say. "I think he's nice." I pick up my binoculars and look toward Brian's roof. "Shhh, he's back."

"Like he's gonna hear," Linda says and then laughs a little. "Jeez."

She tries to grab the binoculars from me, but the strap is secure around my neck. "Hey, you trying to strangle me?"

"Better me than him. Let me see."

"OK, OK. Hold your horses."

I slip the binoculars off and give them to her. She looks. "Where?"

"Over there." I point toward Brian's roof.

"Where? All I see is sky."

"Give 'em to me." Not everyone knows how to use binoculars right off.

I find Brian in the sights and wave. He holds up a sign. *Hi!*

I help Linda focus the lenses, and she finally sees him. "Oh, he's kind of cute."

"See, I told you. Keep watching while I write a sign."

I write: *Hi, Brian. What are you doing?* Then I hold up the sign. I take the binocs from Linda.

Brian is writing, and then I read: *I'm gonna work on my truck.*

Linda grabs the binoculars. "Truck? He's got a truck?"

I shrug. "Guess so."

I write *OK* and hold it up.

"How old is he?" Linda asks. "Probably at least sixteen if he has a truck. And, boy, will you catch trouble for making friends with a teenager."

"Nobody knows, and I don't think he's sixteen."

"He's older?" Linda says with a touch of *Oh my God* in her voice. She shields her eyes and looks toward Brian's house.

"No, I think he's younger. Fifteen."

Linda laughs. "Fifteen, sixteen. You're still gonna catch it."

I look through the binocs again, but Brian has already left his roof.

"He's gone." I snag my cooler of iced tea and take a drink. I invite Linda to help herself, but she shrugs it off.

"Probably went to work on his truck," Linda says. "So now you can go to the playground with me."

"I don't know. I might miss something."

"Like what? One of your sister's stupid UFOs?"

We both laugh, and Linda grabs my hand. "Who cares? Come on before it gets dark."

Polly barks. I look over the edge and see Elaine go through the front gate. She slams it behind her. A black wrought-iron fence stretches across the front of our property. The gate only closes and latches if you slam it, and then it is still a good idea to double-check. Same goes for the side-yard gate. It's a just-in-case rule because of Jelly Bean being outside sometimes.

Linda and I watch Elaine cross the street.

"See." I nudge Linda in the ribs. "You can see everything from the roof."

"It's like spying," Linda says. "It's kind of fun."

We giggle as a green car, a station wagon, slows down on the street near Elaine. A door opens, and she climbs into the backseat.

"Where's she going?" Linda asks.

"That's Diane Rolands's mother. Elaine is probably going over there to hang out with Diane and Sac and whoever else they hang out with."

Linda gives me a shove. "Sac? Who's Sac?"

"Elaine's friend. Her real name is Sarah, but they call her Sac for some reason."

Linda shrugs. "Think they'll have boys over?"

"Who cares?"

Linda does. She is kind of boy crazy. Just about everyone knows she likes Jack DiArchangelo, but she doesn't know that we know. I'm pretty sure Jack doesn't know either. And that's when it hits me. I pick up my binoculars and train them on the park and Scullion Field. Yep, the boys are playing baseball.

"Ohhh!" I say. "You want to go to the park so you can watch your boyfriend play." I give her another shot in the ribs. Jack plays second base for the Clifton Iron Pigs. He is tall, which is always a good idea for a second baseman.

Linda hauls off and clobbers me in the shoulder. "Shhh, no one's supposed to know."

I shrug. "Everybody knows. Even Jelly Bean knows."

Linda looks hurt. She wrinkles her brow and smashes her glasses into her face again.

"Come on, let's go," I say. "Who cares anyway?"

∞

Linda and I scramble up the bleachers on the Iron Pigs' side. We sit behind some sets of parents and kids. Linda points toward second base. "There he is."

Little League spring season is winding down. The Iron Pigs

made it into the playoffs. They are in the field, dressed in their red-and-white baseball uniforms. The other team—the Springfield Rockets—are at bat, and from what I can tell, there are already two outs. A big boy, who must be six feet tall, approaches the plate carrying a bat the size of a small tree trunk. He taps the plate and gets into his stance. Our pitcher, Randy Mulligan, makes the pitch.

Smack! Big Boy wastes no time. He hits a pop-up. Jack signals and makes the catch. Much to the thrill and relief of Linda.

She keeps trying to get Jack's attention, but he never once looks in her direction.

"Why won't he wave?" Linda asks.

"Because he probably doesn't even know you're here. And he's busy with the game. He's…concentrating."

"I guess," Linda says. We stay for two more innings until she says, "Come on, let's go home. I need to have my bike home before dark. My dad'll kill me if I ride at night."

Instead of making our way through the crowd on the bleachers and making everyone mad, we slip under the back railing and jump to the ground. We head toward home, but when we get to the park gate, I stop cold in my tracks because all of a sudden, I am looking right at Brian—without his binoculars and without his roof. He's standing there like he's been waiting for me.

He raises his hand. "Yo."

Linda grabs my hand. "Don't say a word. You might be inviting danger." She sounds just like Officer Wilson when he comes to school and gives us the Mischief Night safety and proper behavior lecture. Boring.

"Aw, he's harmless." I hope.

"Hey, Brian," I say.

"I saw you from over here. I thought you might like to see my truck. I'm rebuilding it… Well, the engine anyway—parts of it."

Linda squeezes my hand. I can feel her heartbeat. Or maybe it's mine.

"I can't," I say in a hurry. "We have to get home."

"That's OK," Brian says. "Maybe tomorrow. I'll be working on her tomorrow too."

I nod.

"Walk ya home?" he asks.

I nod again because I am too nervous to say no and there is hardly a possibility that he has an ax in his pocket.

"Boy, will you catch it," Linda mutters.

She's probably right. I'm a little scared my dad might see Brian if he walks us home, but I'm more scared of going to the home of a boy I don't know. So we head up the hill. I glance at his face and am glad to see that he doesn't have a murderer's eyes.

"So how come you go up on the roof so much?" Brian asks.

"I'm staying there now because of my stupid sister." I'm not ready to tell him about Bud and the sadness in our house and all that stuff. "She's driving me crazy."

"Aw, that's no reason to move to the roof."

"Is if you have my sister. She has this pig—"

"Pig?" Brian stops walking and pulls my elbow. "What?"

"It's a guinea pig," Linda says. "Not an *oink-oink* pig. Joyce has a flare for the dramatic. I heard my mom say that about you once," she tells me.

Brian laughs. "So you moved to the roof because of a guinea pig?"

"Kind of," I say. "It's annoying, and she's always…" I look up the street when I hear the ice cream man. "Forget it. Who's got money for the ice cream man?"

"Not me," Brian says.

"Me neither," Linda says.

"Yeah, me neither."

We start walking again as a bunch of kids push past us to get to the ice cream truck.

"But your folks let you," Brian says. "Because of your sister's guinea pig."

"Yeah. My dad got a little hot under the collar about it. But Mom cooled him down."

"Moms are good for that sort of thing," Brian says.

I smile at him. He has a longish face and really bright, blue eyes. He is wearing the same outfit as before—cuffed blue jeans and a green shirt, along with a pair of heavy work boots. We walk to the top of the hill.

"I guess I better get home too," Brian says. "I'm going this way."

"OK," I say. "See ya on the roof."

"The roof," Brian says, and he takes off running up Crestview.

I wave.

Linda punches my shoulder.

"Hey," I say rubbing my arm. "Whaddya do that for?"

"Because he likes you."

I swallow. "No he doesn't. Not like that. Not like you like Jack. He just likes me because of the roof thing. It's just a thing we have. We're…simpatico." That is another of my new words. I think it is a lovely one.

Linda grabs her bike from the side yard and rolls it to the sidewalk. "See ya tomorrow."

"Guess so."

"Don't fall off the roof," Linda calls as she pedals off toward home.

I watch her for a few seconds, then go inside the house. I need to use the bathroom before settling onto the roof. I am not too crazy about climbing down the ladder to visit the bathroom in the middle of the night.

Mom is watching TV and crocheting. She can crochet anything. We have more crocheted things in our house than they'd have in a museum—if there were such a thing as a crochet museum. We have crocheted covers that slip over toilet paper rolls, crocheted Christmas decorations, and a crocheted toaster cover that my dad hates because he worries about fires. We even have a crocheted toilet-seat cover. It is a blue pond with green lily pads and crocheted frogs. Trouble is, when you push the lid up, the cover doesn't stay up until you sit down because the frogs stick out and keep pushing it back down. They make Dad hopping mad sometimes.

I wonder what new thing Mom is crocheting.

"Hey," I say with a wave.

"Hey," Mom says, not taking her eyes from the TV while her fingers work the yarn. "Thought you were sleeping on the roof."

"I am. I just want to pee first. Jeez."

She doesn't say anything.

I creep like a raccoon past my old bedroom, but Jelly Bean still squeals. I swear, that pig has supersonic hearing. I peek into my parents' room. Dad isn't there. Probably locked in the garage working on his secret whatchamacallit. Nobody, not even Mom, knows what he is building. For a few days after we got the word that Bud went missing, I thought maybe Dad was building something for him—like a wheelchair ramp because there is no way to get into the house except up the concrete steps. I see so many pictures of guys coming home from the war with no legs and stuff. The whole thing makes me so angry, but I can't do a thing about it.

I stand in the hallway and think about the time I broke both my arms at the same time. I was hanging from the monkey bars, and I asked Elaine to give me a push so I could swing. She did. But my hands were so slippery that I fell to the ground. *Smash!* Both arms cracked. I heard them. And then I didn't remember anything else until I woke up in the car on the way to the hospital. Dad didn't make anything special for me, but he did buy me a bunch of fancy straws in all sorts of googly shapes and configurations because both my arms were in casts.

It will take more than straws to help if Bud comes home without legs.

I finish in the bathroom and go straight to the roof. It is dark except for stars and the crescent moon. A perfect night for stargazing. Just like I used to do with Bud. It feels good up here. If I lean back and gaze up at the sky and concentrate only on seeing the stars, I can pretty much feel Bud sitting next to me, pointing at a star cluster, and saying things like, "Right there. That's Ursa Major."

The air is warm and thick—humid. I can see lightning bugs flitting around everywhere. I am surprised they fly as high as the roof.

I settle onto my beach chair and look through my binoculars even though I can't see much except lights in the distance. And I can see the moon, which looks brighter and bigger on the other end of the lenses. It's like I can reach out and grab it, which makes me think about the moon race that the United States is having with the Russians. According to Dad, our countries are trying to see who can be first to get a man to actually walk on the moon. Wow. Walking on the moon. I imagine that for a few seconds. I imagine wearing a spacesuit and taking a step on the moon. I imagine collecting rocks, and then I laugh because I imagine being greeted by an alien—a little green man—and Elaine saying, "See. Told you so, dummy!"

And then I think about my brother, which I seem to be doing nearly all the time lately. I look at the stars and try to find Cassiopeia's *W*, but I'm never sure if I really do. I like to think that I can see the constellations, but sometimes, it's just too hard to connect the dots.

Five

The next morning, the sound of the trash truck making its way down the alley wakes me from a deep sleep. The big, green trucks are always so noisy, and the men yelling at each other around the cans are annoying.

I look over the edge of the roof, and sure enough, the truck is making its way up our alley. A giant, purple teddy bear is strapped to the front of the truck. It makes me laugh. Then I see one of the trash collectors pull a tricycle from a trash pile. "Hey, this ain't bad." But he tosses it into the huge truck jaws anyway.

One of the trash men catches my eye. I wave to him. He waves back and then tosses the Hazels' can back on their lawn. The men never put the cans back in the right place, but no one argues with them about it. Except Cass Duthart.

I go to the side of the roof with my binoculars and see her come out her back door. I zero in on her chubby, pink face just as Peaches dashes between her legs and into the yard, yapping like crazy. I swear that dog will yap herself to death one day.

A trash man grabs Mrs. Duthart's can and dumps it in the truck. He shakes and bangs the can like something is stuck inside. Then he tosses it against Mrs. Duthart's garage door, and that's when the shouting starts. It's the moment I was waiting for.

"Hey, you put that trash can back where it belongs," Mrs. Duthart hollers. "What's wrong with you, you—" And then she uses a word that would get me grounded for a month of Sundays if I ever used it.

Just like they do every Tuesday and Friday, the men ignore her. Mrs. Duthart grabs the can, crams the lid on tight, and moves it to its proper place in her backyard. Then she sees me. Probably sensed me with her secret cranky-neighbor powers.

"Hi," I say, still gazing through the glasses. Even though I know Mrs. Duthart hates my guts through no fault of my own. "How are you?"

"What in blazes are you doin' up there?" she hollers. "You'll break your neck. Does your father know you're up there? And what in tarnation are you doing with those binoculars…spying on people?"

"I'm OK," I say, "and Dad knows I'm here. He let me."

Then she mutters something I can't hear over the sound of

the truck, but I bet it's something against my father because Mrs. Duthart thinks my whole entire family is bat-poo crazy.

I'd rather be bat-poo crazy and live on the roof than sad and dismal like Mrs. Duthart, who has nothing better to do than complain and make trouble and collect balls that just happen to land in her yard. I figure she's collected about a thousand.

Cass Duthart's yard is now a ground-rule double, although everybody hates that rule because it would take no time to jump the fence, grab the ball, and toss it to second base to get the person out. But, like Mom always says, you can't fight City Hall. Or Cass Duthart.

After Mrs. Duthart and Peaches go back inside, I put my binoculars back to my eyes and go searching like I'm the lookout on a tall battleship. But I see nothing out of ordinary. Just some folks leaving for work, I figure. I watch Mrs. Wilbur go into her bomb shelter. Then I see Brian.

He holds up a sign: *Come over and see my truck.*

I scribble on a page of Elaine's sketchbook: *Where do you live?*
5136 Crestview.

My heart pounds faster than a squirrel's, which is 420 beats per minute when it's riled. Did I do something wrong? I know in my soul of souls that if I asked Dad for permission to go to Brian's, he'd have one of his conniption fits and probably ground me until I was thirty. And he'd for sure make me come off the roof.

But something comes over me, and for a second, I don't care if what I am about to do comes with a penalty of death—or worse. Real quick, I write in big letters: *OK.* My stomach knots like a macramé plant hanger because boy, oh boy, have I ever stepped in it this time.

I peer at Brian through the binocs. He waves like a third-base coach sending a runner on to home plate. I wave back and set the glasses in the milk crate. Then I take a deep breath like I am diving into the creek. There is no way in jumpin' blue heck I can tell anyone about going to Brian's house.

Elaine is probably still sacked out. I figure Mom is getting breakfast for Dad. And he is getting ready for work. I climb over the roof edge and down the ladder. The instant my foot hits the ground, I hear such squealing that I jump back onto the lower rung. Jelly Bean. Elaine let her out already.

"Stupid pig," I say.

Polly is in the side yard because it's her job to protect the pig. She barks. Not a loud bark. Just one of her *Don't step on the pig* barks. She does a great job of being a lookout for Jelly Bean. I sometimes see her nose the pig around and even scoot her toward the steps. Elaine swears on a stack of Bibles that Polly even picks the pig up like she's a puppy and carries her to the front stoop. It might be true, but I've never seen it. Just like I've never seen any of Elaine's UFOs.

Mom is in the kitchen whisking eggs in a blue-and-white-striped bowl while Dad sits at the table reading his newspaper, concentrating on the sports pages.

"Hi," I say. "Phillies win?"

Dad snaps his paper.

Guess not.

Mom spins around on one foot. "Oh, Joycie. How was your first night on the roof?"

"Fine." I wait for Dad to drop his newspaper and say he is surprised I didn't break my neck falling off the roof or something like that.

"Hungry?" Mom asks. "Making French toast."

Uh-oh. Mom making French toast is usually a clear indication that she and Dad are arguing again. They argue a lot these days over pretty much anything, including whether it is more proper to say "Turn *off* the lights" or "Turn *out* the lights."

The arguing is probably the reason Elaine got up early and let Jelly Bean out. Dad still hasn't so much as let go of a groan, which is pretty unusual. He's always groaning and muttering when he reads the sports pages, especially since it's looking more and more like the Phillies could make the playoffs if, according to him, they make the right choices.

"Any UFO sightings last night?" I ask, hoping that question will raise my father's interest and lower his paper. But no.

Mom says, "Make sure you brush your teeth after breakfast. I have to go over to Mrs. Lynch's today and sew some hems for her and—"

That's when Dad lowers his paper. He snaps it with a sharp, loud snap. Aha! This particular silent treatment has something to do with Mrs. Lynch.

I back away from the table, hoping I won't miss anything but knowing they won't start again until I'm out of earshot. I can't hang out in the hallway listening because I have to go to the bathroom.

I hurry upstairs. Pee. Then poke my head into my old bedroom.

"Yo," I say.

Elaine is sitting on her bed as usual, with her knees drawn up and her sketchbook resting on them. She is holding one of the precious drawing pencils she makes Dad drive clear into the city to buy at a fancy art supply store. Those pencils are the best drawing pencils in the entire universe, according to Elaine.

"Hey," she says without looking up.

"They fighting again?"

"What do I look like?" Elaine asks. "A war correspondent?"

I open my dresser and pull out a clean shirt, which I change into.

"You're gonna need a bra soon," Elaine says, looking straight at me now.

I glance at my chest. "Am not. I'm fine."

"You're such a tomboy."

"So how come they're fighting?"

"It's stupid as usual." Elaine sets her drawing pad down. "Something about Mrs. Lynch. Dad's all mad because Mom won't charge Mrs. Lynch for hemming her dresses or fixing her collars and stuff. Mom says it's her way to bless Mrs. Lynch. Makes her feel good. Like she's doing something worthwhile."

"So what?"

"So Dad says Mrs. Lynch has plenty to spare and we can use it."

"Well, he is right about that," I say. "But Dad keeps letting customers pay him with brownies and Phillies tickets."

"His choice."

I didn't see why Mom hemming dresses for God was any different than him unclogging toilets for a pound of fudge.

"Come on," I say. "Mom's making French toast."

When Mrs. Lynch was a girl, she was in a fire and got burned all over her face and neck and arms and legs. Mom fixes her dresses with high collars and long sleeves and hems that are long enough to cover most of the scars. Except you can still see them. Like wrinkles. Thick patches on her cheeks and near her ears. Sometimes, they can be hard to look at because they make me feel sad and I wonder what it was like to get burned like that.

"Dad should let her do it," I say on the way down the steps.

"Yeah, I know," Elaine says. "I'm gonna get Jelly Bean."

Dad is already gone when I get to the kitchen. I hear the truck start in the driveway.

"How many slices do you want?" Mom asks.

"Four, I guess."

Mom sets our plates of French toast on the table, and then she sits. She isn't eating—probably already did—but she has a cup of coffee. Mom always has coffee. Morning, noon, night. Doesn't matter. She always has a pot ready. She stares into the cup of pale-brown liquid and then at Bud's spot at the table. She has that faraway look. I watch her, and my chest aches. Ever since the news, no matter what happens around our house, it somehow has Bud on the fringes. Like every upset leads to him. I don't know why that is, but it is.

"Go on," Mom says. "Eat."

Elaine shows up at the table and takes her seat.

"Did you put Jelly Bean back in her cage?" Mom asks.

Elaine nods. She spreads butter and syrup on her toast and digs in like she hasn't eaten in days.

"I'll be home in plenty of time to make supper," Mom says. "Make sure you get lunch and"—she looks straight at me—"you be careful up there today."

I nod as I chew, knowing full well that I am about to embark on a clandestine adventure that involves a boy I met on the roof and his truck.

Mom is wearing her blue paisley dress. Her hair is already combed neatly, and she smells like Vanilla Fields—her favorite perfume. The fragrance reminds me of sugar cookies. She's ready to go. I glance at the clock. Eight thirty.

"Sac and I are going to the mall today," Elaine says. "She needs a new pair of shoes."

Sac is the daughter of two church missionaries. She's staying with the Rolandses while her parents are traveling around signing up people and churches to pay for them to work in Africa.

"Do you have bus fare?"

The bus stops down the block, right in front of Doctor Cherry's house on the opposite end of our row.

"Mrs. Rolands is driving us."

"Take a couple of quarters out of the jar in case Mrs. Rolands takes you to Kresge's for lunch. I don't want to owe that woman."

"Can I take five? I need an eraser."

Mom nods. "I guess Sac will be going back to Africa soon."

"Sometime in August," Elaine says.

Sac's family is only here for what my dad calls a furlough, like they are in the army. Mrs. Rolands says they are in the army—God's army. Although I don't know why God needs an army.

I think Elaine is going to miss Sac when she leaves, and I really, truly feel sad for her. Then I smile because I realize that even the word *missionary* had the word *miss* inside it. Guess it goes with the territory.

Mom sets her coffee cup in the sink and fills a small galvanized can so she can water her plants.

Elaine stares into her plate. The amber-colored syrup and butter swirl like the paisleys on Mom's dress. Maybe like the thoughts and pictures in Elaine's head.

"Sorry about Sac," I say. "That she has to go back to Africa."

Elaine doesn't say anything. But she looks at me, and she doesn't call me *creep* or *dummy* or anything, so I figure her just looking at me is a good enough way of saying thanks.

Six

I couldn't have been a luckier duck if I'd planned it. With Mom heading to Mrs. Lynch's and Elaine going to the mall with Sac, I have it made. All I need to do is wait for them both to leave and then zip over to Brian's house.

Mom waters her African violets. She keeps them on a wrought-iron plant stand with four levels that's under the dining room window. Mom is a member of the African Violet Society, although I never see her go to any of the meetings—if they even have meetings. But she once entered one of the plants in a contest and came home with a red ribbon for second place. The ribbon is still attached to the pot. I watch her pull two dead leaves from one of the small plants.

I still have some French toast on my plate, and it's so good that I want to finish it before getting ready to go to Brian's. So I eat while Mom hums to her plants. But then she says, "So what do you have planned for the day? The playground? Bikes with Linda?"

I swallow a piece of toast sideways and have to wash it down with milk. "No...um... I mean, I don't know yet. Maybe." I'm lying. Mom always knows when I'm lying.

"Just behave yourself," she says. She has her back to me, which I figure is a good thing because if she looks me in the eyes, she'll know for sure I'm lying.

"OK," I say, gulping milk. Then I dash away from the table and head upstairs, leaving a perfectly good piece of French toast swimming in a tiny pool of syrup.

Elaine sits on her bed with Jelly Bean while she waits for Mrs. Rolands. I swear she loves that pig more than life itself sometimes. She coos and talks to Jelly Bean like she is a person or a dog. And Jelly Bean makes sweet noises back at her. Which is kind of weird, except I guess I treat Polly the same way. Sometimes, Elaine holds the pig up to her face and they nuzzle noses. Sometimes, Jelly Bean rides on Polly's back around the house or out in the yard. And she loves black licorice. Weird, I know.

Finally, twenty minutes after Mom heads off to Mrs. Lynch's house, Mrs. Rolands arrives for Elaine.

"Your chariot has arrived," I say when I hear a car horn beep.

Elaine sets Jelly Bean in her cage. "You be a good girl." She gives the pig a scratch on the back.

What does she think the pig will do? Tunnel out of her cage? Then I have an image of Jelly Bean meeting up with other guinea pigs in the alley and plotting some rodent crime.

I stand on the front stoop and wave good-bye. Once they turn the corner down Palmer Mill, Polly and I set off for Crestview Drive.

I don't have any trouble finding Brian's house. His isn't on the end, so I head around back to the alley and see him standing near an old beat-up truck that has the front end lifted up on cinder blocks.

"Yo," he calls. He wipes his hands on a rag, which he stuffs into his back jeans pocket.

"Hey," I call as I walk closer. Polly dances ahead, her tail wagging.

I stand a few feet from Brian and try to make the butterflies in my stomach fly away. I am not having much success. "Is that your truck?" I ask, ignoring the flutter.

"Ain't she a beaut?" Brian says. "She's a 1952 Ford. 'Course she needs a lot of work. But I'll get her running." He pats the fender like the truck is his friend or something. "Have to," he says with a dreamy look in his eyes. It's like Brian's truck is his Jelly Bean.

I move a little closer and run my hand over the driver's side fender. It's hard to tell what color it is—not just the fender but the whole truck. The hood is blue, like a blueberry, with patches of gray and rust, and the door is gray like most of the rest of the truck. But the back part that hauls things is blue like the fender. "It reminds me of a picture my dad showed me of one of his old trucks. He used to fix them up too."

Brian moves around to the front and peers into the engine. "Come see. She's got a six-cylinder, overhead valve engine with a hundred and one horses of power."

"Oh, that's good," I say, not wanting to sound like I know absolutely nothing about truck engines, which of course I don't.

"Sure is," he says with a grin that seems to bubble up from someplace deep inside. "She's a beauty. And as soon as I get her running, I'm gonna take her around the neighborhood and show her off."

"Yeah?" I say. "Does she need much work?"

Brian scratches his head. "Kinda. She was a real mess when we first got her. My brother found her in a junkyard and towed her home behind my father's Chevy truck. He let me steer this truck while he drove the Chevy."

Polly lets out a bark. Brian gives her a quick pat on the head with his nearly black hand. Then he leans into the engine and taps something with his wrench.

"Whatcha doing now?" I ask.

"Gotta replace all the belts and wires and get a new carburetor before she'll run."

"How come your brother ain't working on the truck with you?"

"He can't," Brian says. "He's dead."

I take a step back. "What? No, you're lying to me."

"No I ain't. He got killed in Vietnam." Brian never takes his eyes off the engine while he says it. It's like he is saying something as simple as the answer to two plus two. It also makes me think of Bud for an instant. Just an instant because I can't stand the thought of Bud being dead like Brian's brother.

"Really? But you just got the truck here. How could—"

"Look," Brian says. "It's no big deal, OK? He came home for a little while, we got the truck, and he started fixing it. Then he went back for another tour and got clobbered two days later."

Not a big deal? I think it's a bigger deal than Brian is letting on.

I give Polly a quick scratch behind the ears. "My brother's over there now, except not fighting. He got... He went missing."

"What do you mean?"

"We got a telegram one day that said he had been reported MIA."

"That stinks." Brian finally looks away from the engine. "Mike said it's rough over there."

I swallow. "So when do you figure?"

"Figure what?"

"Figure you'll have her done?"

Brian shrugs. "Gotta be done by July the fifteenth."

"How come?"

"Mike's birthday. I said a promise that I would, and I ain't going back on my promise and…" He looks straight at me. "Then I got somethin' else I gotta do."

I open the driver's side door and climb inside. It isn't very comfortable. The steering wheel is big, and there is a rip in the passenger seat that exposes some yucky-looking foam and cottony stuff. It smells a little like a wet catcher's mitt.

"What do you gotta do?" I ask.

Brian walks around to the window and leans inside. "I'm heading west. Leaving town. I'm gonna drive Mike's truck cross-country to Arizona. Gonna live there for a while."

"Wow," I say. "How come you wanna do that?"

"On account of my dad. He says it will be best for me to finish up high school out there. Gonna live with my aunt Natalie." He taps the door. "But first, I gotta make Mike's truck roadworthy. That's what Mike called it—roadworthy."

I lean my head out of the window. "You old enough to drive?"

"Almost, but I don't care. I'm doing it anyway. I know how

to drive, and that's what counts. Mike taught me. My dad's giving me a hard time about it. But I'll talk him into it."

"Least your brother taught you stuff. All my sister does is play with her guinea pig and see flying saucers."

Brian lifts his chin toward me. "Yeah? UFOs? You mean real UFOs?"

I laugh a little. "Yeah, Elaine sees them all the time. But she sees small ones. And everybody knows spaceships are huge."

Brian laughs. "I guess so. I never saw one, even though you hear about them all the time."

"Aw, they're all just fakes," I say. "Right?"

Brian shrugs. "Who knows? People all over the world claim to see them."

"But why would aliens from outer space come to Westbrook Park?" I shake my head. "Sheesh."

"Why do they go anywhere?"

"So you believe in them?"

"Not really. I'm just saying a lot of people do. Guess your sister is one of them."

I guess, but I still think she is seeing things.

I poke my head into the engine. "What's that?"

"That's where the carburetor goes, if I can ever get the money to buy one."

"Why can't your dad get you one?"

"He would if he could, but I told him I wanna try to do the whole thing myself."

"Maybe you can get your mom to ask him. That's what I do sometimes."

Brian kicks the tire again. "Dead too. Long time ago."

And in that second, I feel a ton of red bricks fall from the sky and pile on top of me. I don't know whether to breathe or not because I never knew anyone before who had a mother die.

"So why's he sending you away? Doesn't he want you around?"

Brian took a deep breath. "He just can't take care of me anymore. I think we're doing OK. But he thinks I'll do better with my aunt because he's always gone. He works two jobs and doesn't make much money…just enough." Brian wipes a wrench with the dirty rag he had in his back pocket. "If I can't get the truck running, he's gonna put me on a Greyhound bus bound for Arizona."

I look into the engine. I don't know about trucks, but from the looks of it, I figure it needs a lot of work. "Maybe the bus would be better."

Brian looks at me and then at his sneakers. "No it wouldn't. I want to drive Mike's truck…just somethin' I gotta do."

And in that instant, I understand. Driving the truck will help keep Mike alive—like Brian hasn't lost all of him. Kind of like being on the roof makes me feel closer to Bud, even though I hadn't planned on that happening. I just wanted to get away from Elaine and the pig and the sadness. I wanted to sit closer to the stars and lean my head back and try to figure out just where the heck Orion was hiding. But then I noticed that if I didn't look away from the sky, I could feel Bud sitting right next to me—closer than the stars.

Seven

N ow what?"

"Now what, what?" Brian looks me in the eye.

"What do you do now? With the truck, I mean." I lean over the engine as far as I can, not wanting to think about dead or missing brothers anymore.

"Gotta get a carburetor. Rebuilt one will do, but they cost money."

"How much money?"

"More than I got. I might be able to pull one from a wreck at the junkyard for cheap. But I gotta get there."

"Why not ask your dad to take you to the junkyard?"

Brian tosses his rag on the ground. And then he laughs. "Nah, he doesn't have the time these days."

I think about it for a second. It's one thing to not have time to go to some faraway junkyard. But another thing to send your kid away.

"How come he says he can't take care of you?"

Brian takes a deep breath and then lets it out his nose like a bull. "He says it's for my own good—to have a female influence—someone who's home all day and can cook and stuff."

I stare into the engine, straight at the place where the carburetor goes. "Still doesn't give him the right."

"What right?"

"To send you away—unless it's what you want."

"Yeah, I guess I do, sometimes. And not being by myself so much would be nice." He looks toward the house and then back at the engine. "I got the new plugs in and even set the gaps myself."

"Good going," I say, even though I don't know what in tarnation he means by setting the gaps. Truck talk. But I can still say *good going* because I can tell it was something that made Brian proud.

"Yeah, but without a carburetor, she ain't going anywhere."

Polly ambles near me and rubs her head on my knee.

"I like your dog," Brian says.

"Yeah, she's a good dog."

"So will ya be on the roof later?"

"Probably on account of I live there now…well, mostly."

"The roof's a good place. Nobody to bother you."

"Yeah, I'll say."

Brian tinkers with the engine a little more while I watch.

Once, he asks me to hand him a wrench. And it reminds me of how Bud used to get me to hand him stuff or get him a soda from the downstairs fridge.

"I better get home," I say after a while. "I'll see you on the roof."

∞

Just as Polly and I cross the street in front of my house, I see Dad drive past. He's headed around the back to park in the driveway. He's home early. Not that it's out of the ordinary or anything. Sometimes, he finishes one job and doesn't want to start another until the next day. I don't know if he saw us or not—and, well, so what? I could just tell him I was down at the park or in the woods with Polly. No need to sweat it. It's just nerves.

I push open the front door and go straight to the kitchen for a glass of iced tea. Man, I'm thirsty. It's so hot. Hotter than jumpin' blue heck is what Dad always says.

I hear his footsteps in the basement and think I might tell him about Brian and ask him to help get a carburetor since Brian's dad is too busy. Maybe he's too sad to help too. Maybe he's even sadder than my dad. Sheesh. A dead wife and a dead son. That's too much.

"Hey," Dad says when he gets to the top of the basement

stairs. He can see me in the kitchen from there. Polly saunters over to greet him.

"Hey, girl," Dad says with a pat on her head.

Polly barks and does a little *welcome home* dance.

Dad nods at my iced tea. "Looks good. How 'bout getting a glass for your old man?" He sits at the kitchen table, looking hot and tired, even for coming home early.

"Been crawling around in a crawl space all morning." He downs his iced tea in one swig. I pour him another.

"Guess that's why they call them crawl spaces," I say.

"Mother home?"

"Nah, she's still at Mrs. Lynch's, I guess."

He shakes his head. "Where's your sister?"

"She went to the mall with Sac and Mrs. Rolands."

I watch as Dad rubs Polly behind the ears. I'm trying to work up the courage to ask about the carburetor.

Dad looks at the clock. "I'm gonna go shower and take a nap. Finished the job early." A moldy smell wafts off him when he stands. His hands are nearly black—like Brian's, only some of the black on my dad's hands is permanent from all the years of crawling around dirty pipes.

"OK, but I wanted to ask you something."

He moves near my mother's African violets and lets out a big, deep sigh. "Mom and her flowers." He stands near the window, looking out, and sighs again. Guess he didn't hear me.

He heads to the steps but stops and looks at the picture of Bud in his army uniform we have on the hi-fi. "Coulda used your help today, son."

I decide not to ask him about carburetors because I'd have to tell him about Brian. Then I'd probably have to tell about Brian's brother, and I don't think I want to tell Dad that news on top of telling him I made friends with a boy I met on the roof. That's probably too much for one dad brain to take.

∞

It's hot outside. Too hot for the roof. Too hot to sit on the roof and think of ways to help Brian get a carburetor. I head for my room since Elaine is out with Sac and the coast is clear. I can rest in my bunk and think.

Jelly Bean squeals like a banshee when I open the bedroom door.

"Just me," I say. "Your mommy is still shopping."

I put my fingers through the cage and give the pig a little tickle. She is kind of cute. I especially like the way her heinie wiggles when she runs. "You don't have any money, do you?"

The pig doesn't answer. I lie on my bunk with my arms behind my head. How could I raise money? I could make a little money by doing errands in the neighborhood. Mrs. DiSipio is usually good for a quarter if I make a mailbox run for her. And Mrs. Burrell might give me fifty cents if I unload her groceries in this heat. But Brian needs more than that. He needs cold, hard cash. And lots of it.

∽

After a little while, I hear a car door slam. Must be Elaine home from shopping.

Yep, she bounds up the steps. Jelly Bean goes wild. Squealing and dancing and wagging her teeny, tiny tail. Like I say, the pig doesn't know she's a pig. Now she thinks she's a dog.

Elaine opens the cage and gives the pig a quick scratch. "How's my little Jelly Bean. Miss me?"

"Gag me."

"I thought you moved to the roof," she says.

"I did. It's just too hot there right now. But I'll go soon enough."

"Told you so."

"Told me what?"

"That you couldn't live on the roof. You're so stupid."

"I can live on the roof. And I'm not stupid, which is exactly why I am not up there now. But I will be."

"Yeah, yeah."

Elaine reaches into her bag and pulls out a silky, whitish blouse.

She holds it up to herself and looks in the mirror over her dresser. "Pretty, huh?"

"Pretty ugly." I jump from my bunk.

"What's with you?" Elaine asks, still looking in the mirror.

"Nothin'."

"Sac and I are going to Sproul Lanes tonight. It's OK because her folks will be there."

"So what?"

"So you can't come. Not old enough. Only for teenagers."

"I don't care."

She sets the blouse on her bed. "Well, it's gonna be fun. Bowling, pizza, sodas."

I smile with gritted teeth. "See how much I care. I got my own thing to do."

"What? Sit on the roof and stare through the binoculars like some kind of Peeping Tom."

"No, better. But I ain't telling you anything."

"Because you aren't doing anything except looking through those stupid binoculars at nothing special."

It takes all my strength to keep from telling her about Brian. But I keep it to myself and smile on the inside.

∽

Mom comes home a little while later, and I hope with all my heart that Dad won't yell at her about helping Mrs. Lynch.

"Think they'll fight?" I ask Elaine. She's on her bunk drawing as usual.

"Who knows?"

"Whatcha drawing?" I ask. I get out of bed and try to sneak a peek.

She quickly pulls her sketchpad against her chest. "None of your business."

"UFOs? Spaceships? Little green men?"

"What if I am?"

"Let me see."

Elaine makes a clicking sound with her tongue. "Oh, all right." She holds up her sketchpad. The ship is pretty amazing. I don't see a driver or anything that looks liked a space alien. The saucer is oval but sleek with a rounded bubble top and lights all around and two long antennas with strange eyes. She colored in the yellow lights with her special crayons she claims were made in France.

"Is that what you saw?" I ask.

"Yep. But no one believes me."

∽

Things at the dinner table are pretty quiet. Maybe Dad is still mad at Mom for helping Mrs. Lynch, and Mom is still mad at Dad for not understanding that all she wants to do is help. Maybe that's where I get it from—wanting to help Brian, I mean.

Finally, it's Mom who speaks first.

"Anything happen at work today?" she asks Dad.

Dad looks up from his plate. "I was just thinking about something I heard at the hot dog stand." He pokes at his potatoes. "John told me his brother Hugh—you know, the brother who was in Nam?"

Mom nods.

"Seems he's not doing so good since he's been back. Real nervous and stuff."

"Oh, dear," Mom says. "I guess it takes time to get used to being home again."

Dad swallows, and then he looks over at Bud's usual place at the table. "Home. I say we make home a real special place for Bud. I say when Bud comes home we have a party. We'll give him a real hero's welcome."

"Is that what he is?" I ask. "A hero?"

"Yep," Dad says. "We should treat him the way we got treated at the end of World War II. Like heroes, like actual heroes. I was even in a ticker-tape parade in New York City."

"For fighting in the war?" I ask.

"Yep. For fighting in the war."

"Wow. I think a party is a great idea." I meant it too.

Elaine pushes her peas around on her plate. "*If* he comes home, you mean. He might never come home."

"You shut up," I say. "He is coming home. You'll see. Real soon. I just know it."

"Now, now," Mom says. "Of course he's coming home." She looks at Dad and says, "So I let the hems out of three of Mrs. Lynch's dresses today."

I guess Dad got over being mad at Mom. He doesn't say a word.

"Must be torture to walk through life with all those scars," she says.

"Nothing wrong with scars," Dad says. "They prove something."

"Like what?" I ask. I want him to look at me and explain how scars prove anything—anything at all. I have a big scar on my knee from where I got cut on an old, rusty stove left out for trash. All it proved was that I got six stitches and a tetanus shot, which I ended up being allergic to. Then Dad rubs his shoulder. I knew it was where he took a bullet in World War II.

"Scars prove you survived," he says, still looking at his plate.

We all got quiet again because I know every single one of us was thinking about Bud and if he'll come home with scars. Maybe some pretty big ones.

We can hardly have a single dinner without everyone's thoughts going to Bud and wondering about him. Sometimes, I think we could start out talking about how much I hate fractions and somehow we'd end up talking about Bud. It all comes back to Bud.

∽

After supper, Dad sneaks away to his garage as usual to work on whatever secret project he has down there. Elaine gets ready for her big bowling night, and Mom stays in the kitchen as usual, washing dishes and fussing with her plants. I head for the roof, even though it's still warm and light enough to go play with Linda.

Every so often, I peer through the glasses—but no Brian. I catch a game down on the field, and I even see Mr. Wilbur go into his bomb shelter. He is carrying a large brown bag. One of these days, I am gonna find a way inside.

A little while later, Elaine brings Jelly Bean outside. Polly is right there with her, nosing the pig around and keeping her from escaping out of the yard. Elaine calls up to me. "Keep an eye on her, will ya? I'll bring her back inside in a few minutes."

I call down. "Sure." I really don't need to keep that close of a watch as long as Polly is on the job. She makes a great shepherd, even though she's a mutt.

I see Brian. He waves. I wave. I write a note on the sketch-book: *How much does a carb. cost?*

He writes back: *$15 at junkyard.*

That doesn't sound like that much money, but I guess for him, it is. And for me. No way I can come up with that much cash.

Elaine returns and gathers up Jelly Bean. She'll leave soon for the bowling party for teenagers. Dad will probably stay in his garage all night, and I'm pretty sure Mom will sit and crochet and watch TV.

∽

The sun is finally down, and the day is starting to cool off, although the air still sticks to my skin. I see Venus come into view and then, blink by blink, a few more stars. I lean back in my beach chair and watch the sky for more stars and more planets and a UFO. One airplane with bright, white lights passes overhead. I think my sister is nuts. If Bud were here looking at the sky with me, he'd think she was nuts too.

The ladder rattles against the side of the house. I jump up, scared at first—until I see the top of a crew-cut head.

"Brian," I say. "What are you doing?"

"I came to visit."

"But you can't. I mean…"

"What? Why can't I?"

He climbs over the ridge, and there he is. On my roof. Plain as day. The skeleton inside my body rattles.

"We can't let my dad see you. He'll get so mad if he finds out I had you up here."

"How come? What did I do?"

"Nothing. It's more because you're a boy for one, a little older than me for two, and, the biggest number three of all, I met you on the roof. Dad will say I could have met any old ax murderer."

"I ain't a murderer." Brian scratches the back of his neck. "Heck, I can't even kill spiders."

"I know, I know. But I gotta keep you secret."

"All right," Brian says. "Your dad sounds strict."

"Kind of strict," I say.

Brian walks toward my little camp. "This is nice," he says. "You got everything you need."

"Yeah. So how come you're here?"

"Just wanted to visit."

I sit on my beach chair. "Sorry. I should get another chair for guests."

"No problem." Brian sits right on the roof. Guess boys don't care so much about getting their pants dirty. Not that I do either, but Brian is already dirty and greasy from working on his truck.

We are quiet for a few minutes, both of us looking up at the stars and the moon. There isn't a cloud in sight.

"Nice night," Brian says.

"Yeah. Pretty clear. Bud and I used to look at the stars a lot. He was really good at pointing out the constellations. I used to pretend I saw them, even though I didn't."

Brian lets go of a soft chuckle. "Yeah. So many stars. Trillions of them. Trillions. Ever wonder what they were for?"

I nod. "Yeah, I have, but I didn't think anyone else did."

"I do. And all those planets too… What are they for?"

"To give us something to look at," I say. "Wonder about?"

"Ever think there could be life on other planets?" Brian asks. "Like your sister thinks?"

This time, it is my turn to laugh. Not because of Brian but because of Elaine. "Well, I think she's nuts. She's always seeing UFOs."

"Yeah, you told me. Ever see one?"

"Me? Nah. Every time I get to the window or look in the right direction, it's gone."

"I wouldn't mind seeing one," Brian says. "For real, I mean. But I guess there really ain't no such thing."

"I doubt it. But boy, if Elaine was right and—" I stop talking because right at that moment the biggest, brightest idea lightbulb of all times lights up in my brain.

Eight

"And what?" Brian asks.

"I just had a brainstorm. A huge brainstorm."

"What?"

"I know how we can get you the money for your carburetor."

"How?"

"Look, Elaine is a really great artist. She can draw or make anything. I mean it…anything."

"That's great, but—"

"I bet we can get her to make a UFO. My dad has all kinds of stuff around, metal and wood and junk, except we can't get into the garage right now… But still, there's stuff in the basement."

"Slow down," Brian says. "What's your idea?"

"It's simple. We build a spaceship and then sell tickets for people to come see it."

Brian really laughs now. He is laughing so hard that he even rocks back and forth. "You're kidding me. That will never work. No one will believe it."

"Maybe not, but…but people are very curious, and if we talk it up, I bet you a million bucks we could raise fifteen dollars."

Brian shakes his head. "I don't know…"

We both look into the sky again.

"My mom always loved the stars," Brian says. "She used to make wishes on them, and she had a knack for seeing shooting stars a lot."

"I bet she'd want us to try."

"Let's do it." Brian breaks into a smile so big, I think his face might crack.

"You mean it?" I say. "I mean, of course. It's a brilliant plan. How could it not work?"

Brian takes a deep breath and continues to gaze at the stars. I liked to say *gaze* as in *stargazing*. It makes the whole thing sound poetic and like you're waiting for something unexpected to happen while you're doing it. And sometimes, it does, like when a star falls from its place and shoots through the sky on a whisper.

We both look into the sky until we hear the garage door. You always know when a garage door is opening.

"My father," I say. "He never opens the garage door, not since he started his secret project."

I go to the edge of the roof and lean over to see if I can see anything.

"Whoa," Brian says. "Careful."

"Trash," I say. "He's just bringing the trash cans out. But it's still weird because he always takes the cans out through the back door."

"Are you sure he's doing something secret in there?" Brian asks, joining me at the edge.

"Yep. It's not the first time. Last year for Christmas, he made my mother two new lamps for the living room."

"That's nice."

"My mother didn't think so."

We go back to the rooftop camp area after the garage door closes.

"He made them out of copper pipe," I say.

"Your mom doesn't like copper pipe?"

"The kind he puts in people's houses. For water to flow through. Pretty weird, huh?"

Brian shrugs. "Maybe he could make the UFO."

"Sure he could. He can make anything, but we can't tell him because we'd have to tell him about you, and I don't think he'd be too happy about it."

"OK, OK, but I'm telling you, I don't know how to make a flying saucer—not a good enough one anyway."

"Look, how about I get you a drawing of one? Elaine's always drawing them. You can start there."

Brian shakes his head. "I don't know. I guess a picture will help. But it's gotta be good."

"Oh, don't worry about that. Elaine draws things so good you'll think they're real."

"Meetcha tomorrow," Brian says, "and we'll get started."

I walk him to the ladder. "You'll see. We'll have people lined up for a mile to see a genuine, bona fide spaceship."

"Bona fide? Don't know how bona fide it'll be." Brian climbs down the ladder.

What I don't tell him is that getting a drawing from Elaine will not be easy. Unless I tell her the plan, and that will mean telling her about Brian and risking her telling Mom. But something deep inside knows I have to try.

I pull my knees up to my chest and think. Before Brian, I felt like I didn't have anything that mattered. Mom has her hems to sew, and Elaine has the pig and her drawings and fancy pencils and paper and erasers. Dad has his secret projects. Bud has the war—maybe not in a great way, but still, he's there because it's supposed to be helping the country, protecting freedom. And now I have something too. I have Brian. I have Brian and a carburetor to buy and a flying saucer to build.

I look up just in time to see a star shoot across the sky.

Yeah, it's good to have something that matters.

Nine

I decide to wait around for Elaine to come home from bowling. I also decide I need to come up with a plan to get her to give me one of her pictures. I can't just steal one because she'd notice the page missing. Asking her could be the best way to go, but I will have to finagle it—that's what Mom calls it when she wants something from Dad. "I'll get him to do it," she says. "But it will take some finagling."

I hear a car pull up.

"Thanks," Elaine calls. "Talk to you tomorrow."

I hurry down the ladder to catch her before she goes inside.

"I need to talk to you."

She jumps about thirty feet in the air. "Hey, creep, you scared me."

"Sorry. Didn't mean to. But I really need to talk to you."

"About what? I'm tired."

"UFOs." I look her in the eye when I say it. You have to keep a straight face when you are finagling.

"Stop making fun of me," Elaine says as she walks to the steps.

"Wait," I say. "It's just…just that I saw one."

"One what?"

"UFO."

Elaine gives me a shove. "Get out. Stop making fun."

"I'm serious."

"Really? You mean you finally saw one?" Elaine's voice is excited.

"Maybe," I say. "I saw something weird—that's for sure."

"I betcha it was the same one I saw," Elaine sounds even more excited. "Tonight. I saw it hovering over the bowling alley. I went outside for some air and there it was, hovering right over the Bowl-A-Rama sign, the neon one with all the pretty colors."

"Did anyone else see it?"

"No. By the time I got Sac and Andrew outside, it was gone. Andrew said I was crazy and there ain't no such thing."

"I saw it." I have to bite my bottom lip to stay serious.

Now, the truth is, I never saw anything except an airplane. But I'm thinking that telling her I saw the flying saucer might help me convince her to give me one of her drawings without asking too many questions.

I'm not sure she believes me.

"Look, I need a favor," I say. "I want you to give me one of your pictures."

"What? Why? You're up to something."

"I'm not up to anything." I can feel my cheeks flush. I always turn red when I out-and-out lie. Even if it's for a good cause. Which this is—a good cause.

"You're always up to something. Spill it."

Elaine sits on the stoop. "Tell me."

I don't want to tell her about Brian. Not yet. "I just want a picture because you're such a good artist, and when you're famous and have paintings hanging in the Louvre, I can show people my drawing and—"

"Aw, you're full of it. That ain't why. Now tell me."

"I can't. Just do it for me. Please. I'll do your chores for a whole week."

"The rest of the summer."

I stamp my foot. "Fine. The rest of the summer."

Elaine laughs. "You're crazy. I'm going to bed."

I climb back to the roof, thinking it is going to be really hard to keep Elaine from knowing the truth—and now I have to do her stupid chores for the rest of the stupid summer.

∞

The next morning, the trash men wake me early with their noisy truck and loud voices. Mom's fixing Dad's breakfast. As usual, he's as quiet as a spider and reading his newspaper. Sometimes, I think he expects to see Bud's name printed inside or a picture of him, so he scrutinizes every page. I shiver.

"Cold cereal this morning," Mom says. "Take it or leave it."

"OK. Corn Flakes." I look at Dad over his paper. "You goin' to work, Dad?"

"Just like every day," he says.

"'Course he is," Mom says. She plops the box of Corn Flakes on the table. "What kind of plans do you have for the day, Joyce Anne? Don't forget, it's almost the Fourth of July."

"Oh yeah, fireworks," I say. "Can't wait. Maybe I'll watch them from the roof."

"No you won't," Dad says with his face screened behind the paper. "You'll be with the family. As always. Besides"—he pulls the paper down so I can see his face—"I might just have something… special planned."

I pour milk over my flakes. "Like what?"

"You'll see. Now eat your breakfast. I gotta go unstop Mrs. Culbertson's sink."

Dad kisses Mom's cheek. He grabs his lunch box and thermos off the counter.

"Do you know what he has planned?" I ask Mom once Dad has gone downstairs. "Is that what he's doing in the garage? Is it for the Fourth?"

"He never lets me in on his projects. Guess we'll all find out together."

I munch down my flakes, thinking it's kind of neat that Dad and I are both wrapped up in projects. I set the bowl on the floor for Polly. She likes to drink the leftover cereal milk. Mom will kill me if she sees.

"Where's Elaine?" I ask. "Still getting her beauty sleep?"

"Nah, she was up. Came down earlier."

I swallow. "Did she say anything?"

"About what?"

I shrug. "Just anything?"

Mom gives me one of her *You're up to something* looks. "Nope. She seems kind of quiet this morning."

When Polly finishes, I retrieve my bowl, drop it in the sink, and go to find Elaine. I find her in the bedroom sketching, with Jelly Bean on her lap.

"Whatcha doing?" I ask.

"Drawing."

"The flying saucer? Really? Let me see."

"Not finished."

"That's OK. Let me see."

She turns her sketchbook around, and there it is…one bona fide flying saucer.

"It's cool," I say. "Can I have it?"

"It's more than cool. It's real. It is the exact one I saw last night. And no, you can't have it."

"Why? What gives? You promised."

She sets the sketchpad aside and puts Jelly Bean back in her cage. "I'll let you have it under one, maybe two conditions."

"But I'm already doing your chores. This ain't fair."

"Do you want it or not?"

I take a breath. Here it comes: sibling blackmail. "OK, what are your conditions?"

"The whole story and nothing but the whole story. If I'm going to give you one of my original drawings, I have to know why."

I take a huge breath and look out the window, thinking I might be able to see Brian on his roof. But I can't. I have no choice. I have to tell.

"OK," I say, turning around like I saw an actor turn in a movie once, just when he was about to announce the murderer. "Now remember you can't breathe a word of this, not a single word of this, to anyone. It's top secret. A triple-sister secret."

Elaine doesn't look at me. She keeps sketching, but she

asks, "Does this have anything to do with what Dad's doing in the garage?"

I shake my head. "No."

"So spill," Elaine says real final-like. "The beans—all of them."

"I met a boy. His name is Brian. He likes to hang out on his roof. That's how I met him. On the roof."

Elaine laughs. And that makes the pig squeal. "Oh, come on. You met a boy on the roof?"

"I was looking through my binocs, and I saw him across the way. On his roof. Over on Crestview Drive. I guess lots of people like the roof...I don't know. But anyway. I went over to his house yesterday and—"

All of a sudden, Elaine takes such a giant breath that I think she's sucked all the oxygen out of the room. "You what? You went to a boy's house? Without permission? A boy you met on the roof? You are crazy...as a loon."

At least I have her attention now. "Yeah, I did. So what's the big deal?" Even though I know it's a pretty big deal—a giant deal—I don't let on. "He's nice."

"Oh man, oh man, are you in for it! Wait until Dad finds out."

"He can't find out, and you better not tell him. Triple-sister secret. You swore."

Elaine hugs her pillow to her chest. "Yeah, yeah, but what does Roof Boy have to do with needing a picture of a flying saucer?"

"I'm getting to that." I sit on the one chair we have in the room. A rickety, old wooden folding chair Dad got at church. You have to sit just so or it will collapse. "Now listen. Brian is fixing up an old truck. It was his dead brother's."

Elaine shoots me a look.

"He died in the war before he had a chance to fix it up himself."

Elaine swallows. I swallow too. "Bud's OK," I say after a few seconds. "I know it. He promised me he'd come home, and I'm holding him to it."

"Mmm-hmm. Right," Elaine says. "So what about this kid?"

"Brian wants to fix the truck and drive it around Westbrook Park to honor his brother and then drive it to Arizona so he can live with his aunt because his father can't take care of him anymore." Phew. That's a lot of information.

"I still don't get what in tarnation that has to do with the UFO!"

"He needs money to buy a carburetor—"

"A what?"

"A carburetor. It goes in the truck engine. And we thought we could build the flying saucer and sell tickets for people to come see it and raise money so he can buy the carburetor and fix the truck before July fifteenth."

Elaine laughs. "Now I know you're crazy. It's like you can't possibly be my sister. Mom got you from gypsies."

"Please," I say. "It's the only way. His brother is dead. His dad can't help him, and to top it off, he's got a dead mother. That's like a triple whammy." I didn't want to tell her that it was important to me too. That I needed something to do, something to care about.

Elaine gets up and paces around the room like she needs to stretch her legs. Then she looks at her drawing. "Look, even if I agreed to your cockamamie scheme, how will you build it?"

"I don't know. We'll put our heads together. I bet Brian can build anything. And Dad has enough junk lying around the house to build a real rocket ship. I figure we could use Christmas lights or something and—"

Elaine pulls herself up to her full height.

"OK, I'll give you a picture on one more condition."

"What? I told you the story."

"One more. This is too big for just two conditions."

"OK, OK. What's the condition? And it better not be stupid."

"You stop calling me *pig nose*."

I sigh. "Aw, man, I like calling you *pig nose*. But, OK, OK. I'll do it. But just for summer."

The door bursts open. "Laundry day," Mom says. "Gather it all up and bring it down. You too, Joyce."

"OK, OK," we say.

Mom stands at the doorway and looks at us. She doesn't ask any questions or say anything. She smiles though. That weird *I know you're up to something* smile she has.

"We'll be right down, Mom," I say.

I wait until I'm sure Mom is all the way down the steps, and then I hug Elaine. "You're the best."

"Yeah, yeah, I hope it works."

"So give it," I say.

Elaine reaches for her sketchbook. "Not so fast. It's not finished."

"It's good enough."

"Nope. I'll give it to you when I'm done."

"Fine."

I look out the window again. And then I say something I didn't plan on saying. "Maybe you should come and meet Brian and stuff. Maybe you can help us figure out how to build it."

"I guess." Elaine looks at her sketch again. "If you're gonna do this crazy scheme, it should be perfect…just like the real thing."

"Bring the picture, and we'll go over to Brian's."

"Now?"

"Yeah, why not?" I say.

Suddenly, I feel nervous about having Elaine meet Brian. I really need her to keep my secret. I hope she likes him.

"Don't forget laundry," Elaine says. "And you can carry mine down too."

"What? You do your own."

She crosses her arms and raises one dark eyebrow in a very sinister fashion. "One of the conditions, remember?"

"All right, all right," I say.

I carry all the dirty clothes to the basement. Mom is already busy with a load.

"Here you go." I say.

"Elaine's too? How come?"

"No reason," I say.

Mom just says, "Uh-huh, OK."

I take a moment to look around the basement. There are stacks and stacks of boxes and stuff. There's got to be enough junk to build one measly flying saucer.

Ten

I head back to the bedroom. "Come on, let's go."

"Hold your horses," Elaine says. "I need to find my other sneaker."

"It's under the bed." Normally, I would make her look all over the house even if I knew where it was, but considering how much I need her, I tell her.

We scramble down the steps.

"Going out, Mom," I call loud enough for her to hear down in the cellar.

"Hold up," she says.

Elaine and I stop cold at the front door.

Mom comes up with a wicker basket of clean clothes. "Where are you two going?"

No way we can tell her where we're really going. Mom stands between the living room and dining room. "I asked where you two are headed."

"Just out," I say.

"Together?"

Elaine drapes her arm around me. "Yeah, together. I'm trying to do what you say, Mom…you know."

Mom gives us a look. But she doesn't say anything. She just turns around and heads back to the kitchen.

"What did you mean?" I ask when we got to the end of the walkway.

Polly barks.

"About what?"

"What you said, about doing what Mom said."

"Nothin', she just said I should humor you."

"That's what she told me about you. Especially when it comes to your UFOs." I skip a few steps ahead of her. Polly stops to sniff around a telephone pole.

"They're not my UFOs. They're from outer space."

I swallow a snicker. If my plan is going to work, I have to convince Elaine that I am on her side, at least a little.

We walk around past the playground and around the corner toward Crestview.

Elaine keeps her sketchbook tucked under her arm. Mom didn't ask about it because it is never strange for Elaine to leave the house with drawing stuff.

Polly sidles next to me. I pat her head. "Let's go up the alley. He's probably out back working on his truck."

The back alleys of row houses are where the kids mostly play. You can get a pretty good ball game going in the alley and an even better game of hide-and-seek—especially at night. I'd say the kids on Gramercy Drive have the best hide-and-seek games ever. One of the big kids figured out how to kick one of the light poles and knock out all the lights on the block for a minute or so. Just enough time for us to scramble and hide in almost pitch-black.

"That's his house," I say. "The one with the green garage door and the truck parked in front."

I am about to knock on the garage door when Elaine grabs my hand. "Listen! It sounds like crying."

I put my ear to the door. I hear a man's voice. Must be Brian's dad. "It'll be OK, son. It's better this way. Just until you finish school."

I hear Brian's voice. "I want to stay here."

"It's just not possible. I… With this new job, I'll be around even less than I am now."

"Why'd you take the job then? I don't want to go to Arizona."

I put my hand over my mouth. He told me he wanted to go. Guess he was just being tough. Like when I say I like going to the dentist, even though I'm scared almost to death.

"I need the money, Brian. And you need a home. Aunt Natalie can give you that."

There was a long silence until his dad says, "Aunt Natalie is buying the bus ticket for the twentieth. I'm sorry. You can't drive across the country in that beat-up old truck."

"We should go," Elaine whispers. "It's their private business."

We start to back away, but first, I sneak a peek through the cracked wood on the garage door. Brian looks toward the door right as I look in. I see him swipe a tear from his cheek. And not just any old tear, I figure. A big one. A tear that carried a whole boatload of sadness.

Elaine grabs my hand. "Come on."

We run as hard as we can toward the park and then stop to catch our breath.

"Do you see?" I ask. "Do you see why I have to help him? His own father doesn't want him." I stamp my foot on the ground. "I hate him. How come he can send his own kid away?"

Elaine and I sit on the field bleachers.

I throw a stick for Polly to chase down.

"I don't think he wants to," Elaine says. "It's just…just that with no mom and with him being gone all the time, he can't take proper care of Brian."

I wince and pull the stick from Polly's mouth. "I thought getting yelled at and grounded and stuff was hard."

"Yeah." Elaine sits her sketchbook next to her on the bleacher. She reties her sneaker, making two perfectly sized loops, exactly the same. She wears pink sneakers with green laces that glow in the dark. She probably got them at the mall—at some store only teenagers shop at.

I toss the stick a few more times, and Polly returns it each time.

"So guess what?" Elaine says.

"What?"

"Maybe I'll help you build that UFO for no charge, no conditions. I want to help Brian."

"Thanks." I smile and lay my head on her shoulder. "Do you ever think about leaving?"

"Leaving what?"

"Home."

"Nah. Not really. Do you?"

I lift my head from her shoulder and toss the stick for Polly. "Sometimes…when I feel like no one cares about me."

Elaine gives me a little shove. "Aw, come on. That's bull. Who doesn't care about you?"

I want to tell her that sometimes, it feels like she doesn't care about me, but I instead, I say, "You're right. I guess everybody cares." But then after a second or two, I say, "It's just…just with Bud missing and—"

"Well, sure, silly. We all have to care about him and worry and get sad and stuff. He's more important right now. That's all."

"Sure. That's all it is," I say. "Let's go see Brian."

"But what if his father's still there? What if they're still talking or Brian doesn't want company?"

"He'll want to see us. He needs us. And besides, nobody can talk about stuff like that for very long. It makes your heart hurt too much."

∞

We make it back to Crestview Drive. I check the front of the house for his father's truck. "It looks a little like Dad's."

"Don't see it," Elaine says.

"Good. Maybe he left."

We go down the alley, and this time, the garage door is open. I see Brian inside. He's wiping a wrench on a greasy, blue rag.

"Hey," I say.

He looks at us, and his face goes red like a McIntosh. "Hey."

"I brought my sister, Elaine."

Elaine raises her hand and wiggles her fingers. "Hi."

"Hey," Brian says.

The three of us just stand there like three mannequins in a store window. I figure he knows we heard and he knows we know and, well, someone has to speak first.

Polly barks.

"Sorry, Brian," Elaine says.

"Yeah," I say. "We heard."

Brian took a breath. "Figured that. I heard you talking. Well, don't sweat it. Ain't nothin'. Not really."

"We're here about the plan," I say. "Elaine and me."

"Yeah, how's that?" Brian walked out of the garage. He kneels down and gives Polly a good scratch behind the ears. I figure that's a good thing. A dog is the best medicine after a big hurt. Polly licks his face twice and lets him nuzzle her head against his chest.

"So how are we going to build this UFO?" he asks. "We don't have a lot of time."

Elaine opens her sketchbook. "This is a drawing I made of the UFO that keeps flying around."

Brian looks at the drawing. "Hey, you're good."

"Thanks," Elaine says.

"No, you're like an artist," Brian says.

"Anyway," I say. "The plan is the same as last night. We build the UFO, like a model, and then we sell tickets to all the kids in the park to come see it. *Bing, bang, boo,* you've got your money."

Brian laughs. "For real? We're really gonna build this space-ship and sell tickets?" He shoves the rag into his back pocket.

"Yeah," Elaine says. "Why not?"

Brian looks Elaine square in the eyes. "Then what?"

"We'll set it up somewhere," Elaine says, "and maybe even hang it from a string or something to make it look like it's flying. People will come."

"Yeah," I say. "Fifty cents a ticket to see an actual flying saucer." I tap the picture. "It's a flawless plan."

Brian smiles and looks at the drawing again. "That's a lot of tickets we'd have to sell."

"Yeah. We can do it," I say. "And Elaine can draw or paint or build anything."

Brian looks at Elaine. "Really?"

"Yep," Elaine says. "This is my first flying saucer, but I bet we can figure it out."

Brian scratches behind his ear with the wrench he is holding. "OK, I'm game. Let's do it."

Eleven

Brian throws open the hood of his truck with a thud and props it open with a stick.

Elaine looks inside at the same time as him. They bumped heads a little, and then they laugh and smile at each other.

"OK, OK, we got a UFO to build," I say.

"Not so simple," Brian says. "I can set the gaps on spark plugs, change oil, and even replace a timing belt—but build a flying saucer?"

Elaine looks at her drawing. "Plans. We need to make plans. You know, like an architect."

"Like a schematic," Brian says.

"Yeah," Elaine says. And they smiled into each other's eyes again, and I got a wobbly feeling in my stomach. I hate romance.

"Come on," Brian says. "My father won't be back for hours. We can work in the garage at the workbench."

Polly settles down in the shade of the truck while we go inside. It smells of grease and dirt and heat.

"So how big do you think it needs to be?" Brian says. "Aren't UFOs like really huge?"

"Not the ones I've seen," Elaine says. "They're about this big." She holds her hands apart.

"About two feet?" Brian says. "Talk about little green men. These must be really small little green men."

"Yeah, pygmy aliens," I say, all of a sudden feeling left out of the conversation.

"I was thinking," Elaine says. "We can use a turkey roasting pan, the kind with the lid. Might have to seal the lid on tight." She points at her drawing. "See, like this." And then she sketches it out.

"Yeah," Brian says. "I can solder them together."

"Good," Elaine says.

"But it needs a top," I say pointing to the drawing. "Like a dome or bubble."

"It's not a bubble," Elaine says. "But it does need a…a thing."

I roll my eyes. *Bubble* is a much better word than *thing*.

Brian and Elaine keep looking at the drawing and then around the garage as though he has spare flying saucer parts just lying around.

"I know," Elaine says. "A Jell-O mold."

"What?" Brian says.

"Yeah. Mom has these copper jelly molds. You know… They make little Jell-O things, like fancy blobs and shapes."

"I've seen them," Brian says. "My mom used to make them too."

"So we get a small one and put it on top." She quickly adds the Jell-O mold to her sketch. It looks pretty neat.

"And I can put a little pipe on the back, like in your drawing," Brian says.

"And it will need lights," Elaine says. "Around the middle."

I think for sure they'd listen to me about the lights because I had already thought about Christmas lights.

"Christmas lights," I say in hurry before either one of them can say it.

"Christmas lights," Brian says like he didn't even hear me.

"Yeah," Elaine says. "They have those small ones now. My dad got some last year. And for the eyes, I can make cardboard cutouts."

I wander outside and sit with Polly until Elaine finally calls me. "Hey, what are you doing?"

"Nothin'." I say.

"We think we got it figured out," Brian calls.

"OK," I say, still patting Polly.

Finally, they come out of the garage.

"We need to figure out how to sneak the supplies out of Mom's kitchen," Elaine says. "And since you're the biggest sneak I know, that's your job."

"No problem. I sneak stuff all the time."

Brian laughs.

"Just bring the stuff when you get it," Brian says. "And I'll fire up the soldering gun."

That's when he and Elaine look dreamily into each other's eyes again. I hate googly eyes.

"Sheesh." I walk on ahead with Polly at my side.

Sneaking the goods out of the kitchen isn't too tough. We do it while Mom is in the basement working on laundry. I stash the roasting pan and the Jell-O mold behind the hedges out front while Elaine goes upstairs to pee and check on Jelly Bean. She never goes out without checking first.

Getting the Christmas lights is a whole other story. The lights are packed away in boxes in the basement, and it is never easy to figure out which box. My father tries his best to keep them organized, but there is just so much stuff in the basement that it's hard to know where to begin.

Mom never throws anything out. She always says, "Don't throw that in the trash. Someone might need it." And so, no matter what it is—a chipped plate, one sock, a set of oddly sized springs—we keep it.

I mix myself a glass of Tang while I wait for Mom to come upstairs. I like Tang. It's pretty famous because it's what the astronauts drank in space. I also snag a chocolate-chip cookie. Mom finally comes upstairs.

"I need you to put all your laundry away, Joyce," Mom says. "And I mean away, proper…in drawers. And then collect trash and bring down any glasses and plates you have in your room."

"Now?" I say. "Can I do it later?"

"Just make sure it gets done."

Mom carries the nearly overflowing basket of clothes upstairs, and I dash down into the basement.

I stand in the room and look around at lots of boxes and old tables, some piles of clothes, and an opened box filled with doorknobs. Another opened box is full of coat hangers.

I pick my way through the sea of cardboard the best I can without disturbing it too much. And then I see it: a box marked *Christmas*.

"Hope that's lights and not ornaments."

I yank it from its spot between two other boxes. "Rats." Ornaments.

Another box. And another. Finally, I find the one with the

lights. But they are the big bulbs. I know Dad bought a few sets of the tiny lights.

And then I find it. The motherlode of tiny lights. *Eureka.* I hold the small green-and-red box and read: Merry Bright. 35-Light Set. Guaranteed to light. "I hope so."

I run upstairs, out the front door, and stash the bulbs with the roasting pan and Jell-O mold. Then I go inside. I find Elaine and Mom in the bedroom talking.

"Just go slow," I hear Mom say. "But I'm glad he's cute."

I swallow. Brian? Were they talking about Brian?

I make a noise, and Elaine looks at me. I give her the thumbs-up.

"Thanks for the talk, Mom," Elaine says.

Mom pats Elaine's knee. "Any time. Now put that laundry into drawers, please, not on the floor." She looks at me. "And you too. And don't forget the trash."

"But, Mom, I have to—"

"What?" she asks.

"Aw, nothin'. I'll put my clothes away."

"And mine too," Elaine says once Mom is out of earshot.

"What? No soap. Put your own underwear away. You said no conditions."

Elaine was cradling Jelly Bean like she was a baby. "I changed my mind."

"You are such a jerk." I heave a huge sigh. "Fine. I'll put all the clothes away, including your stupid underpants and bras."

"Thank you," Elaine says. "And make sure you hang my blouses in the closet so they don't get wrinkled. Keep my panties folded, and put the bras to the left of the panties. I'm going to Brian's. Meetcha there." Bras to the left. I shake my head. What a weirdo.

"Wait a sec," I say. "What did you tell Mom about him?"

"Nothing much," Elaine says. "Well, not too much. I told her I met a cute boy is all. I was trying to stall her so you could get the lights."

"Well, stop talking about him. She'll get suspicious. And besides, he's not your boyfriend. I met him first...not that he's my boyfriend. It's just... Aw, never mind."

"She doesn't know anything," Elaine says. "Don't be such a worry wart. And I never said he was my boyfriend. But maybe you want him to be your boyfriend."

I chuck a rolled-up pair of black socks at her head. Only I miss and the socks bounce off her shoulder and ricochet onto Jelly Bean, who is still resting in the crook of Elaine's arm.

"Hey, cut it out," Elaine says. "You'll hurt her."

"I didn't mean to, and you know how Mom is. She has a way of finding things out. It's spooky. I swear she has ESP."

Elaine chuckles. "Yeah, like the time she knew I played hooky that day before the school called her. How could she? I hung out with Grace DePalma all day, except for going to the mall." Elaine shakes her head. "There was just no way she could have known."

"She has special powers. I bet she'll know I took the lights."

"Of course she will. I bet you a million bucks she'll decide to roast a turkey today and make a Jell-O mold. But we can't worry about that. We have a UFO to build, and you have laundry to put away and trash to collect."

"Yeah, yeah," I say. "I don't know why I have to get the trash. I've been on the roof."

Elaine shrugs and smiles.

"I stashed the lights and stuff behind the front hedge." I'm not looking at her when I say it. I'm too busy shoving shorts in her drawer. "How many pairs do you need? Sheesh."

But she is gone. I hear her pig-nose voice drift up from downstairs, telling Mom to bring Jelly Bean in the house in a little while. I quickly finish with the clothes, then collect the trash into the bag Mom left and dash down the steps.

Mom is watching her favorite cooking show on the TV. The chef is talking about whipping egg whites. I wonder why Mom watches cooking shows. She's already a great cook.

"Take that trash out to the can," Mom says.

"Aw, Mom, but—"

"No buts. Just do it."

Man, oh man, I want to get to Brian's before they start building the flying saucer, so I run down the cellar steps two at time. I stop just long enough to check the garage door. No soap. Still locked. Dad is getting ready to reveal his latest project, and the joint is still locked up tight.

I drop the bag into the can, cram on the lid, and dart into the yard through the side-yard gate. I hear the latch click, and since I'm in a hurry to get to Brian's, I keep going without making the double check.

I keep an eye out for Jelly Bean because I don't want to step on her. I see her munching on a large dandelion leaf near the peach tree.

"See you later, Jelly Bean," I say as I dodge through the front gate and slam it behind me.

I run down the street. I get just to the mailbox when I hear squealing. Not happy squeals. Loud, blood-curdling squeals.

My heart pounds. I run back to the house. The squeals grow more blood-curdling.

"Jelly Bean!"

I throw open the front gate and stop—frozen.

Twelve

Bubba, the huge, white German shepherd from across the alley, had gotten Jelly Bean.

I scream.

Bubba grabs her by her wiggly, little heinie and tosses her in the air like a toy.

I scream.

Jelly Bean flails in the air. I see every action like it is in slow motion. Her little legs move like she is trying to run away.

I scream.

Jelly Bean crashes to the ground with an awful thud.

Polly—where is Polly? It's her job to protect Jelly Bean, but she's not in the yard.

"Polly! Polly!"

I run toward Bubba. "Get out. Get out of here."

Bubba snatches the pig up in his mouth and looks at me with

wild eyes. The hairs on his back are standing on end, his ears are pulled back, and white foam drips from his jowls.

I pick up the only weapon I can find—a jagged, fist-size rock—and am just about to throw it when I hear another scream. It's Elaine.

I throw the rock. It barely makes the dog flinch as he shakes Jelly Bean side to side.

I run at him and kick him.

He drops Jelly Bean.

She lies on the grass wiggling and shaking.

"No, don't come near here," I scream to Elaine. But that's like holding back a burst dam. I start to cry. I want her to go back to Brian's. I don't want her to see. I try to hold her back, but she breaks through my arms.

She pushes Bubba out of the way like he's a puppy, picks up Jelly Bean's limp body, and holds the pig to her cheek.

Bubba growls. I holler at him. "Get out. Get out!" I make a move toward him. He lets out a yelp and runs through the side-yard gate.

The gate.

It is swinging open.

I swallow a lump the size of Bubba in my throat.

I look at Elaine and the pig. Jelly Bean is still alive but barely. I can see her little body rise and fall with each tiny, painful breath.

Elaine sobs. And sobs. "No. Nooooooo. Please don't die."

My mother and Polly burst out of the house. "What happened? I heard a dog and..."

"It was Bubba," I say.

Elaine drops to her knees. Jelly Bean is still making noises, but they keep getting fainter. "Please don't die," Elaine cries. "Please don't die."

Polly nuzzles Jelly Bean. She lets out a low whimper and looks Elaine straight in the eyes.

Tears run down my cheeks. "Please," I whisper. "Don't die."

I listen for the pig noises. I listen until the noises stop.

I swipe the tears from my face. I don't deserve to cry. It's my fault.

"I don't understand," Mom says, looking straight at me. "How'd Bubba get in the yard?"

"It was me," I say. "I didn't check the gate. I thought it was closed tight but...but—"

"You?" Elaine says through an ocean of tears and sobs. "You left the gate open?"

I throw myself into my mother's arms. "I'm sorry. I'm sorry."

My mother squeezes me around the waist and tells me to sit on the stoop. "I need to help Elaine right now."

I sit on the step. My entire body trembles. "It's my fault. I was a hurry."

My mother kneels near my sister. She tries to take Jelly Bean from her, but Elaine won't let go. "Maybe she's not dead. Take her to the vet, Mom. Doc Evans will fix her."

Polly sits on her haunches and lowers her head. She whimpers and whines.

Mom reaches for Jelly Bean. This time, Elaine lets her go.

"I'm sorry," I say. "I'm sorry." But no one hears.

"Come on, honey," Mom says, taking Elaine's hand. "Let's go inside." She looks at me with hurt eyes. "You too, Joyce Anne."

But I run. I run hard and fast. I run toward the playground. I run through the baseball field, not even caring that there is a game. I run straight through the infield, even though people holler. I don't care. I slip through the hole in the chain-link fence and slide down the hill into the woods. My palms scrape against jagged rock. I run and dodge the trees and vines snaking along the ground. I trip over rocks and branches and keep running until I can't run anymore. My sides ache as I suck air into my burning lungs.

I lean against a large rock and cry. I killed Jelly Bean.

Thirteen

Salty tears run into my mouth. But I can't even wipe them away. My arms are folded so tight around my stomach. I can't move because I will crumble into a million pieces if I budge one inch from this rock. I feel the jagged edges in my back, but that's all I can feel. Jagged edges and…and what? I can't name it. It's a feeling so big, I cannot contain it in a single word. *I killed Jelly Bean.* The words bounce and echo in my brain.

If only I had checked the latch. It was the rule. The one rule. And I ignored it because I was in such a hurry. Such a stupid, dumb hurry to get to Brian's house.

My sobs come harder, and for a moment, I think someone might hear. But there's no one around. Not now. The woods are empty. Except as I catch my breath and ease my cries, I can hear the rustle of the tiny animals under the dried leaves on the ground. I set off walking, heading to the creek where the water tumbles and falls over rocks and branches and the hideous sofa some idiot tossed into the water. I probably know every inch of the creek. I follow it for as long as I can, clear down to the old factory.

It's an eerie place. The buildings are full of cracked windows from kids chucking rocks at them. It's abandoned now.

Maybe I should move into the factory and live with the raccoons. I don't know if I can ever go home. Not now. My head is pounding so hard that I stop walking, and my legs fold like a wooden chair beneath me.

I hear Polly barking to beat the band.

"Polly girl, you found me." I clap my hands, and she runs toward me, tail wagging. She licks my face. I wrap my arms around her and…I cry. I sob into her warm fur. She lets me. She just lets me.

"I didn't mean to do it," I say. "I-I know I should have checked the gate. It's the rule. I know it."

Polly barks and pushes against me. I know she wants me to go home. I know she is trying to tell me it's OK. But it isn't OK.

I pat Polly's head.

I have to face Elaine now. I have to tell her how sorry I am. How can I ever be sorry enough?

There isn't enough *sorry* in the world to make a dent in the huge mountain of forgiveness I need.

Polly barks. She uses her high, almost shrill bark, which is her way of telling me it is time to go home and that's final.

"Come on, girl." My stomach goes wobbly when I stand. "I messed everything up."

The trudge home is slow. I take the long way around Palmer Mill and up Briarwood before turning onto my street.

When Polly and I reach our house, I stand on the front sidewalk. My heart pounds, and my hands pour sweat. I can hear Jelly Bean squealing in my brain, and for a second, I hope she is still alive. Miracles happen, don't they? Maybe Mom saved her. She once saved a baby robin by having Doc Evans amputate its leg on account of it was busted. Another time, she got a piece of stuck, pink gravel out of my red-eared slider's throat before the turtle choked to death. And she was good with people too. All the neighbors called on my mom when someone got sick or if a mom wasn't sure if her kid needed stitches or not. Mom knew. She always knew. She always makes thing better when no one thought they could. Maybe even...this.

I start to get a little excited, thinking that maybe, just maybe... until I see Dad at the door. His face is stern. Sterner than ever. He pushes open the screen and stands on the top step. I can't move. He's been watching for me.

"Elaine's very upset," he says.

I swallow as tears well in my eyes.

"Wh-where's Jelly...Jelly..." My bottom lip quivers.

"Mom put her in the basement. I think that dog broke every bone in her body."

I fall into my father's arms.

"It was a mistake," he says. "A big mistake—but a mistake just the same."

I pull away from him. "I'm sorry. I-I—"

"There's nothing to say, Joyce. Just come inside and we'll get through this."

∞

The house is quiet. Real quiet. The TV is turned on, but the sound is so low, I can hardly hear it. Dad sits in his chair while Polly curls up on the couch. She will miss Jelly Bean.

And Elaine? So much will be different now. Instead of getting up every morning, opening Jelly Bean's cage, and giving the pig a quick scratch behind the ears, she'll need to find something new to do. Instead of sitting with Jelly Bean in the yard while she sketches, Elaine will be alone. Instead of squeals at night, there will be silence. So much of Elaine's life was wrapped around the pig—I never knew until now.

I find Mom in the kitchen. She's making supper. Looks

like some sort of tuna casserole. Smells like some sort of tuna casserole.

"Are you thirsty?" she asks.

I nod because I can't speak. Every time I open my mouth to say words, the tears start.

"Go on, sit at the table. I'll get you some iced tea."

I sit in my usual chair. Mom sets the glass in front of me. "You can have one cookie if you'd like. You missed lunch."

I shake my head. I'm not the least bit hungry.

Mom goes back to the stove while I sit there with my iced tea. It's good. I am thirsty.

"So what happened?" Mom asks. "You know the rules—especially the gate."

It is like a punch in the stomach. "I'm sorry. I didn't double-check. I heard the latch, but I didn't check." I sit at the kitchen table and wipe beads of condensation from the iced tea glass.

Mom opens the oven and shoves the casserole dish inside. She sets the little yellow egg timer. It looks like an egg, a bright plastic egg. "Twenty minutes or so." Then she sits at the table and squeezes my hand. "What was so important that you didn't check the gate?"

I hear my father in the living room snap his newspaper in agreement.

I swallow another lump. "Here's the thing," I say. And then I tell her everything. About Brian. About the truck and the carburetor and how he is going to Arizona and about the flying saucer. I finish telling her, and then I look her square in the eyes and say, "I was in such a hurry get to Brian's that I didn't check the gate."

My father's paper snaps again.

Mom pats my knee. "Guess you learned a lesson."

I nod about a dozen times.

"You know what you need to do," Mom says.

"Elaine?"

"Yeah, you need to talk to her when she wakes up."

Tears pour down my cheeks again. "What do I say?"

"Mostly that you are sorry—but after that? Well, it will take time."

I take a breath. "What about Jelly Bean?"

"Oh, we'll have a funeral, you know, like we did when Humbert the hamster died. That will help."

I drain my glass of iced tea and set it near the sink.

"Thanks, Mom," I say.

Then I hear an even louder snap, and a big blustery sound comes from my father.

"He's really mad at me," I say.

"Disappointed, Joyce. There's a difference."

I don't feel the difference.

"We have rules for a reason," Mom adds.

"May I go to the roof now?" I look past my mother and out the dining room window.

"Supper will be ready soon."

"I'm not hungry."

"You'll still come down and sit at the table. That's an order. And, Joyce, let's forget about the UFO caper, OK?"

"But what about…" My eyes close like they do when you know something deep inside but don't want to let it out. I look away from Mom. "OK. Fine."

I head toward the front door.

I don't look at Dad because I know I'll cry if I even glance in his direction. And because I know there are no words I can say that will make him not be disappointed. He can't tell me what to do to make it right. I hear the blustery snap of his newspaper. I have to figure out how to make it right on my own.

∞

I get my binoculars and look straight toward Brian's. Yep, there he is. He waves. I wave back, only with not as much gusto as usual.

He holds a sign: *What happened?*

Aw, man, he doesn't know about Jelly Bean or that I told

137

Mom about our plan. We were supposed to be at his garage earlier to get started. Before…before the pig died.

I quickly write in big, red letters: *I need to talk to you.*

I watch him through the lenses. He shrugs and then holds up the *OK* sign.

We make plans to meet at the playground after supper. Now I have two disasters on my hands.

∽

"Joyce Anne, time for supper." My mother is calling me from the side yard.

I climb onto the ladder and start down to the spot where Bubba attacked Jelly Bean.

"Where's Elaine?" I ask when I get to the kitchen.

"I'll get her," Dad says. "You sit."

The thing about my father is that sometimes it's hard to tell how much of what he is saying sounds the way it does because he's angry or because he's sad. Whenever we talk about Bud, I hear that mixture in his voice. But he can't be angry with Bud. It isn't his fault he went missing. So Dad must be angry at the United States Army. But at the same time, I hear sadness around the edges of each of his words, almost like his words are tiny dams holding back a whole torrent of tears.

Today is like that, where Jelly Bean is concerned. Dad loved the pig too. I'd catch him petting her and feeding her dandelions and black licorice from time to time.

Mom sets the tuna casserole on the table. She always calls it Tuna Terrifico. But not today. It's so quiet in the house that I can almost hear the steam rising from the hot dish. "It will need to cool," she whispers.

Next, she pours iced tea. I think we drink iced tea with every single meal during the summer. And my mom makes really good iced tea. She has a special way of making it. She steeps the tea in a pot on a stove. That's what she calls it when she puts twelve tea bags—always twelve tea bags—into the boiling water. She lets their little tags hang over the side of the pot like tiny white shirts hanging out to dry.

After the tea steeps for a while, she adds sugar and stirs until all the crystals are melted, and then she squeezes the lemon into the mixture. Always a real lemon. (She tried that fake stuff once that comes in the container shaped like a lemon and is called ReaLemon. I thought Dad was gonna throw a conniption fit.) Then the last step is to pour the tea into a pitcher and add cold water and ice. I figure I could make it if I had to.

∽

After a few minutes, Elaine and Dad come to the table. Elaine looks awful—like she has been crying her eyes out for hours. She doesn't look at me—not really—not more than a glance. And inside that glance are about a million sharp daggers.

"You should eat, honey," Mom says to Elaine.

"Not hungry," she says as she slides into her seat directly across from me.

Dad picks up plates and starts doling out the tuna and noodles and stuff. He uses his fingers to push a few noodles back onto the spoon before they drop on the table.

I am thinking three things:

1. I should say something to Elaine.
2. How do you apologize over tuna casserole?
3. What good was *sorry* anyway?

I try.

"I'm sorry, Elaine," I say with my fork stuck in a chunk of tuna that might as well be Elaine's heart because that's how I feel—like I stabbed her in the heart. I shudder and pull the fork out of the fish and look at her even though she isn't looking at me. "It was a mistake, OK? I-I should have checked the latch."

Not a word. She only stares into her plate of gooey noodles.

"I really am sorry." Unwanted tears stream down my cheeks. I look at my father. He doesn't say a word and neither does Mom. "I'll make it up to you. I promise."

I move noodles around my plate. Yeah right, how on earth could I make it up to her?

Mom looks at Elaine. "Go on, sweetie. You need to eat."

Elaine still stares into her noodles and doesn't say a word.

My mother starts to talk about how Mrs. Lynch asked if Mom could reupholster an old chair.

Dad shakes his head and says, "She paying you?"

"She'll buy the fabric and stuff." Mom says this with her eyes still on Elaine as though she's expecting Elaine to explode into a bajillion tiny pieces and she wants to catch her just before the explosion.

Dad swallows and sips his tea. Then he says in a forced cheerful voice, I guess because he is trying to lighten things up, "That reminds me. Lloyd Bertino called. He asked me to serve on a special deacons' committee. See about getting a new steeple finally."

I shake my head. More projects for Mom. More projects for Dad. And Elaine? Well, everyone is sorry for Elaine. But for me, there is no more project. And my parents don't have any pity left over for me either. They've spent it all on Bud and Elaine.

Somewhere inside, an angry feeling starts to bubble up, and I think I understand my dad just a little bit more. I'm not angry at Elaine, but I'm angry. Angry at me. Angry at Bubba. Angry at the whole situation.

"I said I was sorry." I say this into my plate.

Then I sneak a look at Elaine. Her eyes are filled with tears. She's rearranging her tuna and noodles and peas into a picture of sorts—probably a guinea pig or a flying saucer. I think about Brian and our flying saucer. I drop my fork and push my chair from the table. "I'm not hungry."

I run out the front door and head straight for the playground. I sit on the bleachers to wait for Brian. We will make plans. Plans to build the UFO, have the display, buy the stupid carburetor, and then head west. I want to go with him.

∞

It is still hot, although some dark clouds are moving in. A huge, bottom-heavy thunderhead looks ominous. Rain won't matter to me. I sit and fold my arms tight against my chest, and then I rest my head on my knees and wait for Brian.

"Hey."

I look up.

"How long you been sitting here?" Brian asks.

All of a sudden, I have to fight back tears. "Not long."

He sits next to me. "So what gives?"

"Mom says we have to call the whole thing off. But I don't want to."

"How come?"

"Because of something I did. Because I made a big, fat mistake."

"What happened? Did your folks find out or somethin'?"

I shake my head. "Worse."

"Worse? What is it?"

"I...killed my sister's guinea pig. Elaine is so upset."

"Wow, that's rough," Brian says. "What did you do? Step on the pig? Drop it?"

"She liked to run around the yard and eat dandelions and sit in the sun like a cow. She was safe as long as Polly was out there to watch her and as long as the side-yard gate was closed tight and... and that's what happened."

"What happened?"

"I left the stupid gate open, and a stupid dog got in and...and..."

"Oh man," Brian says. "That's pretty awful. But it ain't all your fault. It was the stupid dog's fault."

"But he got in the yard because I didn't check the gate. We always check the gate. And this time, I didn't. I was sure I heard the latch click. And I was in a hurry to get to your house and start on the UFO."

"Oh." Brian stood. "So...so it's really my fault."

"What?" I look up at him, shielding my eyes from the setting sun. "How can it be your fault?"

"Because I'm the one who needs the carburetor."

I don't know what to say about that. "Yeah, but I was the one who left the gate open."

Brian smiles in a nervous way. "I guess it's really my father's fault. He's the one sending me to my aunt Natalie, and that's why I needed the carburetor in the first place."

"Or maybe it's the war's fault. If your brother hadn't... hadn't..." I can't say the word *died* because it's like if I do, it will somehow jinx Bud.

Brian nods. "He'd be here fixing the truck with me."

I look out over the baseball diamond. A swirl of dust kicks up around the pitcher's mound as a breeze begins to blow. The kind of breeze that signals rain. The kind of breeze that tells the birds and squirrels it's time to go home, to take shelter. The sky is darkening, and I hear a crash of thunder in the distance.

"It's all connected," I say.

"What?" Brian says. "What's connected?"

"Everything. Everything is connected if you keep looking. I left the gate open because it was connected to the flying saucer, and the flying saucer was connected to you, and—"

"Oh, I get it," Brian says. "Everything gets connected. Nothing happens unless something else happened first."

"Yeah, and the more connections you make, the farther away your problem gets. Except…well, except it still matters, it still hurts, and you could make the fault land on anyone or anything. But the part that is connected to you is all that matters when you're in the thick of it."

Brian lets go a soft sigh. "You're pretty smart for a kid."

"I want to go west with you," I say in a hurry.

"What? You mean like run away?"

"I have to go. I can't stay here. Not now. Not after what I did."

"My aunt won't buy two bus tickets. And without that carburetor—"

I'm hoping Brian isn't just humoring me the way I humor Elaine about her UFOs.

"We can still make the UFO and sell tickets," I say.

"I thought your mom said we couldn't."

I shrugged. "We need to make the money for the carburetor. And we'll keep it secret."

Rain falls. Small drops at first, but then all of sudden, it pours down in big, heavy drops—the kind you can see, the kind that splash on the bleachers.

"Come on," Brian says. "Let's run for the shelter."

I look across the playground at the large, green-roofed shelter where we play box hockey and where the recreation director has her office and where she keeps all the pimple balls and basketballs inside a locked cage.

"No, I better not. I better go home. I'm in enough trouble now as it is."

"Suit yourself," Brian says. "I think I'll hang under the shelter."

I take off running toward home. Toward home—toward a different shelter that at the moment feels pretty leaky. But I stop halfway up the hill. Rain drips off my nose. The roof. No way they'll let me sleep on the roof in the rain. My situation has just gone from bad to impossible.

Fourteen

The rain is pouring down pretty hard as I run up the hill toward home. I see Joey Patrillo. He and his two cousins are playing in the street, stomping in puddles and laughing like a pack of hyenas.

"Hey, Joyce," Joey calls. "Sister see any more ships from outer space?"

One of the other boys—I think it's Beezo—punches his shoulder. "'Course she did. She always sees them." Then he makes what I think are supposed to be flying saucer noises.

I get to the house and look to the roof. I'm certain my little island is under water. It's good that my books and other things are inside the tent, but I know I left the binoculars out and maybe a few other things. For a second or two, I think about climbing up there and checking on things. But a crack of lightning changes my mind. I stand on the stoop and take a deep breath like I am about to dive into the deep end of the pool. I push open the door.

Mom is crocheting on the couch, and Dad is nowhere in sight. I guess he's in the garage working on his Fourth of July surprise. I think my dad forgets about troubles while he is working on his projects.

"Hi," I say to Mom.

"You're soaking wet. Go upstairs and change."

"Is Elaine up there?"

Mom nods.

Polly lets out a bark, so I pat her head.

I go to the kitchen first and get a glass of water. Then I poke around a little, pretending I'm busy when I'm really just trying to avoid going upstairs.

But I can't do this forever. Especially after Mom tells me to get changed for the nineteenth time.

∽

I stand outside our bedroom for a pretty long time. The door is open, and I can see Elaine sitting on her bed, drawing as usual. I swallow hard—Jelly Bean's cage is still there. Elaine has tied a black ribbon around it.

"I'm sorry," I say.

My sister shrugs without so much as a glance my way. My heart sinks into my sopping-wet sneakers. "I...have to get changed."

She shrugs again.

It doesn't take me long to change into another pair of shorts and a shirt. I leave my wet clothes in the bathroom, and then I stand in the hallway. I just stand there feeling like I have nowhere to go. It's a cinch Elaine doesn't want me in the room. So I head downstairs and go straight for the front door.

"Where do you think you're going?" Mom asks.

"The roof."

"No. Not in a storm. You stay inside tonight."

"But, Mom, Elaine is so mad and…"

"Doesn't matter. You stay in. Read a book or something."

∽

That night, after everyone has gone to bed, the house is quieter that it has ever been. Quieter because my brother isn't home to bang on his drums or watch TV all night. Quieter because there are no guinea pig squeals. And quieter because Elaine won't speak to me.

I hear her sniffling into her pillow, and all I can think is that I need to find a way to replace Jelly Bean and then leave for Arizona with Brian.

For a while, I listen to the rain and watch the dancing shadows that are even more sinister than usual tonight. Elaine stops sniffling. The room is warm, so I jump down from my bunk.

Now, since we don't have to worry about rain coming in, I open the window and look out at the still-cloudy sky. Just one star, off in the distance, hangs like a diamond between two small, dark cloudy spots. Even the moon is shrouded.

"Starlight, star bright," I whisper. "First star I see tonight. I wish I may, I wish I might have the wish I wish tonight." Then I close my eyes tight and wish with all my heart that Elaine will be OK and start talking to me and that I can find a way to make her feel better.

And then it comes to me.

"Elaine," I call in a loud whisper. "Look. It's…it's a flying saucer. Elaine."

I shake her. She doesn't wake up right away. I shake harder. "Elaine. It's a flying saucer."

"Where?" she says as she sits up.

"Outside our window."

"Stop making fun of me. Haven't you done enough?"

Finally. She is talking. Believe it or not, I am happy she is angry.

"I'm not making fun. It hovered right in front of the window and blinked its lights like…like you know… What do they call it? Morse code."

"Oh yeah, what was it saying?"

"I don't read Morse code but…but I think the Martians—"

"I never said they were Martians."

"Whoever. Aliens. I think the aliens were telling me to tell you I was sorry again and…to tell you I'll do anything to make it up to you."

Elaine pulls the sheet up though it's still as hot as blazes outside and inside. The little fan we have in the room isn't doing much except blowing the hot, swampy air around. "You can't."

I climb back up to my bunk, wishing I was climbing onto the roof.

∽

And that is exactly what I do the next morning. I wake before Elaine. The sun is on the rise. The rain is gone. The storm has passed, and even though it didn't last long, at least I got Elaine to say more than a single word to me, more than a grunt. I decide to take that as a good sign. After I use the bathroom, I change into yellow shorts and a blue shirt. I tie my still-wet Keds onto my feet and slip out the front door without even saying good morning to my mother.

I head straight for the ladder, and lickety-split, I climb to the roof to survey my camp. It isn't as bad as I thought it would be. The rain left a few puddles, but the tent is still standing and my books and other things are safe under the canvas. But the sketchpad I use to write messages to Brian is destroyed. Water-logged. My binoculars don't seem any worse because of the storm. Although I know Dad will kill me if he finds out I left them in the rain.

After cleaning off the lenses with my shirt, I take a look. Brian isn't on his roof. I scan the neighborhood and only see the mail truck and a few folks milling around. Mrs. Wilbur is hanging clothes to dry on the line near the survival shelter.

After a few minutes, my stomach growls, and I think I had better head down for breakfast. The last thing I should do is make Mom angry.

∞

Mom has bowls on the table and boxes of cereal—Corn Flakes and Rice Krispies.

"Did Dad leave for work?" I ask.

"No, he's in the garage working on his surprise."

I pour Rice Krispies into my bowl. "Mom, can I talk to you about something?"

"Sure," she says. "What's up?"

I push my cereal down into the milk. "It's about the flying saucer exhibit."

"Yes, we agreed. You are going to forget the whole silly thing."

I swallow, wondering how to tell her I still want to build the flying saucer and have the exhibit. But then she starts talking about Jelly Bean.

"We will have Jelly Bean's funeral today."

My heart sinks into my sneakers. I chew my cereal, still thinking I should tell her about the flying saucer plan. And I might have done just that if Elaine hadn't walked into the kitchen carrying her sketchbook.

"Good morning, honey," Mom says. "How are you feeling?"

"Sorrowful, Mother. I feel sorrowful." Elaine sets her sketchpad on the table. It's open. She's been working on a pencil drawing of Jelly Bean in a pasture of grass and dandelions. The dandelions look odd though. They each have a tiny eye drawn into the jagged leaves.

"What's with the eyes?" I ask.

Elaine pours milk over her Corn Flakes and ignores me.

"Dad stayed home for Jelly Bean's funeral," Mom says. "But we should have it this morning in case he wants to go do a job."

"I made a cross and a little tombstone," Elaine says.

Of course she did. I would have helped if she had just asked me.

"Why don't you girls finish up with breakfast, and we'll have the service in the side yard before it gets too hot."

"We should bury her under the peach tree," I say.

Elaine slams her fist on the table. "It's not your choice!" Then she cries and wipes her face with a paper napkin. "Does Jerkface have to be there?"

"No name calling," Mom says, "and of course Joyce Anne needs to be there."

Elaine grabs her drawing book and runs for the stairs.

I push my bowl away as that angry burble in my stomach comes back. So what if we have to bury Jelly Bean? So what if Elaine doesn't want me there? Maybe I won't go to the stupid funeral.

But right then and there, I make my decision. I am gonna go ahead with the flying saucer display and get Brian his carburetor. Just as soon as the funeral is over, Brian and I can get started, and we'll make enough to buy Elaine a new pig too. Then everyone will stop hating me. Especially when I'm on my way to Arizona.

Polly and I head out the front door. She goes straight for the side yard and sniffs around the spot where Jelly Bean died. I go straight for the ladder. But before I start to climb, I pat Polly's head. "I didn't mean for the pig to die. I'm not a cold-blooded murderer."

Polly barks and licks my face.

"You just tell them I'm on the roof when they come out for the stupid funeral."

I read *Alice in Wonderland* and wait for them to come out and bury Jelly Bean.

I get to the part where Alice meets the Cheshire Cat.

"How fine you look when dressed in rage," the Cheshire Cat said. "Your enemies are fortunate your condition is not permanent."

My angry feelings start to fade.

Alice's rage wasn't permanent and neither is mine. Elaine's might not be either. Or my dad's. Maybe he won't always be angry about Bud.

The sun is a little higher in the sky. I wonder if the sun is up in Germany or if it is still night.

"Joyce Anne, are you up there?" my father calls.

∞

The only other funeral I have ever gone to was the one for Humbert the hamster. He died from natural causes, and it wasn't nearly as sad as this.

Elaine stands near Mom. She's all dressed up in her new blouse and green shorts. She used poster paint to paint a daisy on one cheek. She's holding a small cardboard box painted with flowers and trees and dandelions. She must have hand-decorated it last night. *Jelly Bean* is painted in gold on two sides. I stare into the small, guinea-pig-size hole Dad dug under the peach tree. A small mound of dirt waits nearby—dirt that we'll use to cover the box.

Polly is wearing a black ribbon around her neck. She sits on her haunches between Mom and Elaine.

Dad is wearing his plumbing clothes—no shirt-and-tie or black. It isn't that kind of funeral, at least for him. "Today we are here to say good-bye to our friend and pet, Jelly Bean," he says.

Polly nuzzles Elaine's leg.

And that is when Elaine loses it again. "She was a good pig," Dad continues. "And we will all miss her." Then he clears his throat and looks at me. I suppose it is my turn to say something.

I have to sniff back tears as feelings of guilt well up inside again. All I can think to say is "I'm sorry" and "She was a good pet." There had to be something better to say. But I can't think of it. I look into Elaine's swollen, teary eyes. I can see how much she loved Jelly Bean. A shiver wiggles through my body.

Elaine's lower lip trembles. Mom drapes her arm around her. I close my eyes and wish my father would put his arm around me.

"Jelly Bean was the best pet and a good friend," Mom says. "Remember how she loved peanut butter and black licorice? Remember how she rode on Polly's back?"

Polly whimpers and nuzzles the decorated box.

"Yeah," Dad says. "She was not your average guinea pig."

"She was one of the family," Elaine says. "My best friend."

"Yeah," I say. *Yeah* is a pretty stupid thing to say.

Elaine sniffs. She kneels and places the small, decorated box into the hole. "I'll miss you forever." Then she wipes some dirt over the top of the box.

We all stand there. No one moves, no one says a word for what feels like an hour. Finally, Dad says, "I think we should all get on with our day."

And that is that.

∽

I can't stand the thought of hanging around anymore. So I head toward Brian's. I am going to earn some money to buy a carburetor and a pig and make things right.

On the way past Linda Costello's house, I have an idea. Maybe Linda can help. She can help round up kids to come for the exhibit.

Now the thing about Linda Costello is that she will do practically anything for red licorice. I once got her to stand in the middle of the street and cluck like a chicken for three red licorice whips.

I see her bike in the yard and figure she's home. So I knock on the door. Linda doesn't live in an end house like me. She is sandwiched in between like a giant slice of baloney.

Her mother comes to the door.

"Oh, Joyce. Go on up, honey. She's in her room."

Her bedroom door is open, and her favorite music drifts into the hall. The Monkees. She loves the Monkees.

"Hey," she says.

I close the door and whisper, "I need a favor."

"Oh, no you don't," Linda says. "Not another one of your favors." She is sitting crisscross-applesauce on her bed and looking through *Tiger Beat* magazine. "I'm not doing anything for you. I always get in trouble."

"For red licorice?"

"How much?"

"Ten whips."

"Must be big. What do I have to do?"

I sit down on her bed. "The first thing you have to do is promise not to tell a word of this to a living, breathing soul under penalty of death."

"OK, OK. Don't give yourself a heart attack."

"I'm serious. Pinkie swear." I hold up my pinkie finger, inviting her to lock hers onto it as a solemn oath of secrecy.

"Jeez," she says. "So dramatic."

"Good—now listen." I make sure the door is still closed and turn the music up a little.

And then I tell her. I tell her about the flying saucer exhibit, and I tell her about Jelly Bean. Telling about the pig is the worst.

She stares at me through her thick glasses. "Oh wow," she says when I'm done. "Oh wow."

I feel my eyes burn with tears. I sniff them back the best I can.

"Elaine loved that pig more than…more than she loved you, I think."

"That's why I have to buy Elaine a new pig."

"How you gonna do that?"

"I just told you. The UFO exhibit."

Linda tries not to laugh, but she can't help it.

"Don't laugh. It's one of my best capers ever. It will work. And Brian needs our help. And I need your help…for Elaine."

"I don't know anything about flying saucers," Linda says. She flips a page of her magazine. "But I feel bad about the pig."

"Yeah, I feel so bad, I don't think I can stand it. That's why I need your help."

She smashes her glasses into her face. "I don't know."

"Look, I think Brian and I can build the thing by ourselves all right. What I need you to do is round up some kids…lots of them to come see the exhibit."

Linda laughs a little. "You're cracked. How am I supposed to do that? With a lasso?"

"I don't know," I say. "Tickets. You can make tickets and sell them. Fifty cents each."

"I don't know."

"Just write on pieces of paper. UFO Exhibit. 5136 Crestview Drive. It's easy."

"If it's so easy, why don't you do it?"

"Because you're a much better artist than me. I'll give you the ten red licorice whips, and I'll throw in a box of Dots."

"OK, but if I get in trouble—"

"Never happen," I say on my way out the door. "Just make the tickets."

Fifteen

As I round the corner near the park, I see Bubba sniffing near some chokeberry bushes. I freeze. I've never been afraid of him before, but now my entire body shakes. "Bubba," I call, even though I'm so scared.

He looks my way and then goes back to the bush.

"Bubba," I call again.

This time he darts toward me.

I back away.

He stops and sits on his haunches, his tongue lolling out to the side. His eyes are wide and black. He pants.

"Why did you do it? Why? You stupid, dumb dog."

I want to kick him. But then I remember something my mother said one day after Polly chewed her way through an entire Easter ham. She said, "She's just a dumb animal. She didn't know that was our dinner."

"You just a dumb animal? Is that why you killed my sister's

Jelly Bean? I hate you. Go on. Get outta here." I pick up a rock and...and I'm about to throw it at him when all of a sudden, I throw it down the street. Bubba runs after it.

"Go on. Chase the stupid rock. Chase it."

∞

Brian's garage is open. He is standing near the workbench holding the flying saucer. It looks almost exactly like Elaine's drawing.

"I found the stuff in the alley. Elaine must have dropped it when...you know, she heard Jelly Bean." He holds the UFO up for me to see. There is a small dent in the bottom. "I did the best I could. Like it?" he asks.

"It's really neat. You built it by yourself?"

"Uh-huh, I had to...you know, for Elaine. So you can buy a new guinea pig."

"What about the carburetor?"

"Maybe that too, but if not, I can take the bus."

"But I'm going with you, remember? You have to fix the truck."

Brian sets the saucer on the workbench. "I've been meaning to talk to you about that."

"About what?"

"Going to Arizona with me. I'm...I'm not sure that's a good idea. I could... We could get into trouble."

"But, Brian…" I start to feel scared again. Scared or something. "I have to go."

Brian nods.

"I got Linda Costello making tickets to sell," I say.

"Good idea. Now we just need to set up the display." Brian glances around. "My father thinks we're nuts, but he said we could have the display here in the garage." Brian picks up the flying saucer.

It really is nice. He even put lights on it.

"I couldn't make the eyes though," he says. "And we'll need to plug the lights in to get them to work, but I figured maybe we can hide the wires somehow."

"Sure," I say. "We can figure out something."

Brian snags a wrench from the wall and slaps it into his palm. "Is she OK?"

"Elaine? Yeah, well, sort of. She cries a lot. I think she hates me. No, I *know* she hates my guts." I kick at a stone and send it flying out of the garage.

We set a black backdrop up against the wall. Brian had painted a large piece of plywood with black spray paint. "It's supposed to be the night sky," he says. "I was hoping Elaine would paint stars and planets on it to make it look even more real."

I shrug.

Then we hang the flying saucer from the ceiling using fishing line. You can't even see the line. The UFO looks like it is actually flying…well, as long as you use your imagination. Next, Brian exchanges the regular white lightbulb in the garage for a black light, and that makes the scene look even eerier and more bona fide. Not that I know what a flying-saucer scene should look like. But I can use my imagination.

The whole time we work, my heart's desire grows stronger and stronger to not only help Brian but to make everything better for Elaine.

"We'll need some kind of music," Brian says. "It will help with the illusion."

"Yeah, but not the Monkees."

"No, something classical. My mother used to listen to it all the time. I bet we can find something in her records. Come on. Let's go look."

Brian's house smells funny, like the trash hadn't been taken out in weeks. I see piles of newspapers and laundry. Dirty socks strewn around and dishes with dried-up food.

On the coffee table is a picture of a guy in uniform. He looks like Brian, only older. It is the only thing in the house that isn't covered in dust. I imagine Brian's father wiping the dust off the picture with his hand and then placing it back on the coffee table like it is a priceless work of art. I guess maybe it is.

I run my finger around the frame. Someone killed Brian's brother. I wonder if before he died, he killed someone else's brother who killed someone else's brother and it goes on forever.

I wonder if Bud has killed people—not because he wanted to but because that's what soldiers do. Like dogs kill little pigs.

A small cloud forms as Brian blows about an inch of dust off a stack of records. "Berlioz," he says. "Now this is some strange music."

"Never heard of him," I say, moving a stack of newspapers to sit at the dining room table, which is covered with dishes and laundry and mail.

"Hold on," Brian says. "This is perfect." He shows me a bright-blue album. "My mother loved to listen to this guy… Gustav Holst."

"Gustav." I laugh a little. "That's a funny name."

"No, he's great. Mom loved this. The name of the album is *The Planets*."

"Wow, guess that's it."

"Yeah, listen."

Brian opens the lid on an old portable record player with built-in speakers. "This was my mom's too—the record player, I mean. She carried it around the house and listened to her music in every room."

"Do you miss her?"

"Sure I do. What kind of lame-brain question is that?"

"I'm sorry, I didn't—"

I guess it is a dumb question, but I think I just wanted to know if he misses his mom like I miss Bud or he misses his brother...or something. Sometimes, you just want to know that someone else has the same feelings as you.

"It's OK." Brian lifts the record player's needle arm. It looks like a small snake with one tooth. He sets it down gently on the record. "This part is called 'Jupiter.'"

The room fills with sound. It's weird and wonderful at the same time. It starts out bright and starry, and then it sounds far away. But the music comes rushing back like the notes are leading a thousand flying saucers toward Earth. When I close my eyes, I can see them just as Elaine describes them—spinning and spinning and zooming through the Milky Way. Now the music is marching, and I envision the aliens marching toward Earth. They are happy. Very, very happy.

"It's exactly what we need," I say.

I look at Brian. His eyes are closed, and he is swaying a little with the music and tapping his fingers on the wall in perfect rhythm.

"I'm sorry about your mom and your brother. I'm sorry

about your dad and how he has to send you away. I'm sorry you need a carburetor."

Brian opens his eyes. "Thanks. I'm sorry about the pig."

Sixteen

After Brian and I set up the record player in the garage, I say, "I better go check and see how Linda is doing with the tickets."

"Hold on a sec," he says. "Let's light her up first." He plugs in the Christmas lights and the saucer lights up. You can see the cord, but Brian says with the lights off, no one will notice.

"I hope so," I say. "It's gotta be lifelike."

Brian smiles. "Lifelike? You do remember it's fake."

"I know, I know. But it still needs to fool everyone."

"No problemo," Brian says. "It'll do the trick."

On my way to Linda's, I stop at my house first to use the bathroom and…and maybe I want to check on Elaine. Maybe I want to tell her I'm sorry again. Maybe I want to stand in the yard on the spot where Bubba killed the pig. I don't know why I want to do all that, but I just do. And so I run.

The wind is kicking up as I make my way down the street. I think it could rain every day this summer. Something about the mixture of humidity and heat and stuff makes a perfect recipe for thunderstorms.

I look for the sun behind the clouds. It's already on the other side of our maple tree. Sheesh. That means it's getting near supper-time. Brian and I worked a long time. But I can still stop at home and then check on Linda.

I sprint through my front door and up the steps—but stop cold when my foot hits the hallway floor. I hear Elaine crying. I peek around the corner. Mom is holding Elaine's head against her shoulder and petting her hair. "It's OK, honey. These things take buckets of tears sometimes. Buckets."

Buckets of tears. I suck in a deep breath as my own tears threaten, and then I tiptoe past the room, wishing for the gazil-lionth time that I had checked the gate.

"Joyce Anne?" Mom calls.

"Just going to the bathroom."

But instead of going to the bathroom, I run out of the house. I run like crazy all the way down the back alley to Linda's house.

She is standing near her garage door, which is painted like a giant purple-and-white checkerboard. She is wearing purple and white also—purple shorts and a white shirt. She blends right into the garage.

"Did you get them finished?" I huff and puff.

"Yep. Got 'em in this shoe box. Where's my licorice?"

"Yeah, yeah, you'll get your licorice. After the display. And after I see the tickets."

"And Dots."

"Only if there's enough money left over."

"Hey, that ain't fair," she says. "You promised me a box of Dots."

I lift the lid off the shoe box. Inside are a bunch of little pieces of paper. I pull one out.

FLYING SAUCER EXHIBIT

50 cents

The real thing

5136 Crestview

"They're OK." I riffle through them. "Some are drawn better than others." Maybe her hand got tired.

"What do you mean? They're all great. I worked really hard on them." Linda puts her hands on her hips. Guess she really meant it.

"They're not Dots worthy," I say. "But thanks."

She punches my shoulder.

"Let's go," I say. "I think we should start at the park." I put the lid on the box.

"Hold your horses. I gotta tell my mom I'm leaving."

"Did you tell her what you were doing?"

She socks me in the shoulder again. "'Course not, dummy."

I stand under the maple tree with the shoe box, waiting for Linda to get back, when Joey Patrillo rides past on his bike.

"Hey," I holler, running after him.

He screeches to a stop. "What gives?" he asks.

"Want to buy a ticket?"

"A ticket to what?" He keeps riding but slow enough that I can walk beside him.

I show him a ticket.

He stops pedaling to read it. Then he laughs. "Is this one of your sister's gags? She's so weird."

"No, it's not a gag. We found a flying saucer down by Indian Rock. It must have crash-landed."

"Yeah, right. Were there any little green men?"

"No, they must have gotten another ship to pick them up."

Joey laughs. "You're cracked."

"But it's true. We have the saucer, and we're gonna put it on display tomorrow at two o'clock at that address. In the garage. Won't know for sure unless you come. Unless…"

"Unless what?"

"You're afraid."

"I ain't afraid of nothin'. 'Specially some dumb, fake flying saucer."

Joey reaches into his pocket and pulls out a quarter and a dime. "All I got is thirty-five cents."

"I'll give you a discount." I drop Joey's thirty-five cents into the shoe box and hand him a ticket. "Tell your cousins. Nobody gets in without a ticket."

Joey pedals away. "OK, OK," he calls.

Wow, our first sold ticket. This is going to be a breeze. Who could pass up an opportunity to see a bona fide flying saucer?

Linda comes out her front door. "Ma says I gotta be home by supper."

"Just sold our first ticket," I say.

"To who?" Linda asks.

"Joey Patrillo—but for thirty-five cents."

"But we're charging fifty cents." Linda walks on ahead.

"I know. It was all he had, and I figured thirty-five cents was better than nothing. And besides, he'll tell all the other kids."

I skip to catch up with her. "I think we should go to the playground first."

"OK." Linda jumps and smacks the stop sign at the end of our block. "Guess we'll find kids there."

Most of the kids in Westbrook Park go to the playground on summer days for recreational activities—that's what they call the games and stuff they have us kids doing during summer vacation. I usually play box hockey or basketball. Elaine likes the swings. Ever since I fell off the sliding board and cracked my front tooth, I keep to the ground.

Linda and I take our time walking to the park. There's a baseball game going, which means there'll be parents hanging around. And I don't think it's a good idea to sell tickets while the moms and dads look on.

"Yeah," Linda says. "We'll get arrested for selling tickets to a fake exhibit. I think it's called fraud."

"Nah, never happen. But we could get in trouble. I say we go up to the playground and sell to the kids on the swings and playing basketball."

As usual on a muggy summer day, the playground is chockful of kids. I figure this is gonna be a snap. But it turns out to be a little harder than I counted on. For one thing, not many of the kids have extra money. At most, they might have a few nickels or quarters for the candy store. The ice cream truck comes by every day after supper, and that wipes out allowances pretty quick. So buyers are scarce. The littler kids aren't interested, and the bigger kids kind of laugh.

Still, we manage to raise four dollars there. Not nearly enough for a carburetor, but it's a start.

Nicky DeLuca bought two tickets: one for himself and one

for his brother. Scott Worley bought a ticket, but he laughed harder than most of the kids.

"I guess we've sold all we're gonna sell here," Linda says.

"Yeah, and seven bucks and seventy-five cents ain't enough. We need to wait for word of mouth. They'll be lined up down the block to get in. But let's go to Brian's," I say. "Tell him the news. And maybe word of mouth will start up."

"Word of mouth?" says Linda. "What's that?"

"You know, it's when one kid tells another kid and that kid tells another and so on down the line."

"Oh, like whisper down the lane."

"Kinda," I say. "I bet we get a hundred kids to come to the display."

I grab Linda's hand. "Come on. Let's go."

We run through the playground gate and start up Crestview. That's when we see Beezo and Rat, Joey Patrillo's cousins riding down the street on bikes.

"Hey," Beezo hollers, "where's the fire?"

"No fire. We're going to finish getting the display set up."

"Display?" Rat says. "What display?"

Beezo punches Rat's shoulder. "You know the one. The one Joey told us about. The flying saucer they got holed up in a garage. They say it crash-landed down by Indian Rock."

"Not just any old flying saucer," Linda says. "A bona fide one."

"Yeah, yeah," Beezo says. "So if it crash-landed in the woods, how'd ya move it? Flying saucers are pretty heavy."

"The little green men helped them," Rat says. Then they both laugh.

"Look," I say. "Do ya wanna buy tickets or not?"

Beezo digs into his pocket. "I was savin' this for the candy store, but—" He drops three quarters into my palm. "For both of us."

"That ain't enough," Linda says.

"Yeah, you owe me twenty-five cents," I say.

"Cheese-a-loo," Rat says. "Here." He gives me a quarter.

"Thanks," I say. "See you at the display tomorrow. And tell everybody else."

Beezo waves his hand.

"They'll tell everybody," I say.

"Why do you say that?"

"Because they don't believe us."

⚬⚬

We get to Brian's house. He's working on the truck.

"Hey," I say.

Brian looks up from the engine. "What's shakin'?"

"Going great," I say. "We sold some tickets."

"Yeah," Linda says. "And we figure word of mouth will start up, and pretty soon, all the kids will know. We'll be selling tickets at the door."

Brian smiles. "I sure hope so. Elaine needs a new pet."

I suck in a deep breath and wonder for half a sec whether it's right to replace Jelly Bean. Brian can't replace his mother or his brother.

"What's in the box?" Brian asks.

"Tickets and money," I say. "It's not much. Eight dollars and seventy-five cents."

Brian looks away. "Not enough."

"I know. But we'll sell more, and like Linda says, we'll sell tickets at the door. You'll see. We'll get enough money to buy the pig and for you and me—"

"Right," Brian says. "Arizona."

Linda's eyes grow to the size of tea saucers. She doesn't know my plan to go with Brian.

"So we'll open the display tomorrow?" I say.

"Sure. Sooner the better."

Linda grabs my hand and practically pulls me down the street. "So what gives?"

"What do you mean?" I stop. She's still holding my hand.

"You and Brian? Arizona? What gives?"

"Oh that. It's nothin'. Just a mistake."

"You're planning to go with him. Boy, oh boy, are you gonna catch it. You're crazy. You can't go to Arizona."

"Look, I don't *want* to. I *have* to."

"How come?"

"Because of what I did. That's how come."

"You mean Jelly Bean?"

"Because it's my fault she died. It's my fault Elaine got so upset, and it's my fault nobody…"

"Nobody what?"

"Nothin'." I take off running toward home, the coins jingling in the box.

Linda chases after me.

I don't stop until I get to my front gate.

Linda comes panting up behind me. "I wish you wouldn't go."

"I got to. I can't stay here. Elaine hates me now."

"How do you know? Did she say it?"

"No. But…but she won't talk to me. Nobody will."

Linda and I stand near the peach tree. "I wish you wouldn't go. Maybe you can just stay on the roof longer."

"Nah, the roof isn't far enough away."

I suck in a deep breath before opening the front door. I don't see anyone at first, just Polly lying on the couch, asleep and snoring to beat the band. She wakes up when I close the door.

"Hey, girl," I say. "Where is everybody?"

After checking the kitchen, I run upstairs. Elaine is sitting on her bed as usual, drawing. At least she's not crying.

At first, I pretend to need something out of my dresser, and to not look too stupid, I change my socks.

"We decided to go ahead with the UFO display," I say.

Elaine just keeps sketching.

"What are you drawing?"

She pulls the book against her chest. "None of your business. Shouldn't you be on the roof or something?"

Jelly Bean's cage is still on its table. Black ribbon and all.

"Brian made the UFO look terrific. You should come see it. It's spectacular. We even have music. Some dead guy…Gustav something or other. It's really good. Please come."

She shrugs and then erases something with the gummed eraser that came with her set of ultra-fancy drawing pencils.

I wait a little bit. But she doesn't budge.

"Fine." I stamp my foot. "Be mad at me. Everybody is mad at me. But it's not like I did it on purpose, you know. It was an accident."

"No it wasn't," Elaine says. "Murderer."

Wow. My heart breaks into a million pieces.

I run out of the room and down the steps. I don't even stop to talk to Polly or check in with Mom or see about supper. I can't stay in the house one more second. I climb to the roof and cry. I cry until I can't cry anymore. I cry fifty buckets.

Seventeen

The next morning arrives with bright sun swimming in a sea of orange and pink and purple sky. It is going to be a good day. A clear but hazy day. Hot as usual, thick and humid. The kind of day that makes a kid sweat just standing still.

I climb down the ladder through the peach tree branches, which are full of baby peaches. After a quick visit to the bathroom, I go to the kitchen, where Elaine is eating a bowl of Rice Krispies. Mom's fussing with her African violets. She's humming.

"Hey," I say.

"Morning, Lamb Chop," Mom says. "Rice Krispies this morning."

Lamb Chop? Maybe she's not mad at me anymore. I pour myself a bowl. "Today's the day," I whisper to Elaine.

She doesn't even look at me.

"Today's the day for what?" Mom asks.

"Nothin'," I sit in my chair with a flop. "I was just

wondering if today was the day she'd talk to me. More than just three words."

Elaine makes a noise and looks away from me. I guess the work I did the other night to get her to talk didn't last very long.

"It takes time," Mom says.

∽

I finally head over to Brian's house, a little late because I had to do chores—dusting and vacuuming the living room. When I get to the alley, I can hear that Gustav guy's music. And there is already a line with Joey, Beezo, and Rat in the front.

"Come on, Joyce," calls Beezo. "Open up."

"Hold your horses," I say. "I gotta make sure it's ready."

I knock on the garage door. "Brian, open up. It's me."

The garage door opens just a few inches, enough for me to slip under. It's like walking onto another planet, what with the music and the black light and the flying saucer hanging there, seemingly hovering with flashing lights. It's spectacular. Brian even painted planets on the backdrop. He did a pretty good job.

"That's Saturn," he says, pointing to the planet with rings. "And Neptune and Mars. Makes it more authentic, don't ya think?"

"Truly bona fide," I say.

"Still wish Elaine could have painted them," he says.

I lightly touch one of Saturn's rings. "Yeah. Me too."

"Guess we should open the garage," Brian says.

"No. Not all the way. We should let just a couple of kids slip under, to get the full effect."

"Good idea." Brian opens the garage enough for me to slip out again.

"Come on," Joey says. "Let us in."

"If you want to see the saucer, you have to slip under the door," I say. "Give me your tickets first."

Rat is the first, followed by Joey and Beezo and then Wayne Cowsill and David Hazel.

I sell tickets to six more kids who show up out of the blue— must be word of mouth.

Linda Costello shows up. "Let me in," she says.

"You need a ticket," I say. But I'm just kidding. Linda doesn't need a ticket. Besides, she can make her own.

Rat and Beezo and Joey slip back under the door from outer space.

"It was pretty cool," Beezo says.

"Yeah," Joey says. He socks my shoulder. "Better than I thought."

After that, all the kids are hollering to get in, and the music gets louder and louder until—uh-oh—trouble comes marching down the alleyway.

My mother and Elaine are heading our way.

"Oh rats," I say so loud everyone hears me.

I slip under the garage door.

"Brian," I say. "My mother is coming. We need to close down."

The kids inside all holler. "Hey, what gives?" Wayne said. "We just got here."

"You're kidding," Linda says.

"I want my money back," holler a few of the kids.

"Yeah, this is like a fraud or something," says Kathy DeLuca. Her brother James looks like he's gonna punch me or something.

"Sorry," I say. "Can't be helped. Circumstances out of our control."

"Go on," says Brian. "Everybody out."

The kids slip under the door.

Brian turns off the music and then closes the garage door from the outside.

Mom marches through the crowd that scatters around Brian's truck. "Joyce Anne, what on earth are you doing?"

"It's not about earth," hollers Beezo.

"See, Mom," Elaine says. "I told you she was still doing it."

"But, Mom," I say. "We did it for a good reason. We had to."

"That's right," Brian says. "And it's my fault too."

"You must be Brian," Mom says.

"Yeah." Brian looks straight at Elaine with those googly eyes he gets every time he sees her. "I heard about Jelly Bean. That's why Joyce wanted to go on with it."

"What gives?" Kathy says. "We want to see the UFO."

"Not today," Mom says. "All you kids, go on home now. Scat."

The kids scramble, even though a lot of them never get to see the display.

"Aw, Mom," I say. "You don't get it. We...I...we did it for Elaine this time. I mean, it's her flying saucer and, well..."

"She wanted to use the money to buy you a new guinea pig," Brian says.

"I don't want a new guinea pig," Elaine shouts, backing away a couple of steps. "I want Jelly Bean. And you can't get her back." She stomps off down the alley.

Mom moves closer to me. "It's too soon, Joyce."

That angry-sad sensation builds up inside me again. I run after Elaine and grab her arm. "I said I was sorry about a gazillion times. I am not a criminal, and you have to stop treating me like I'm one. And...I was just trying to help by getting you a new pig, but if that ain't good enough, then...then I don't care." I stomp my foot on the ground. "I am not gonna say I'm sorry anymore. Not one more time."

I stare down at my Keds. "I just wanted to help."

Elaine gives me a shove. "I still hate you." She runs off toward home.

I turn toward Brian's house and run smack-dab into my mother.

She holds my shoulders. "I told you not to do this."

"I had to do something," I say. "I had to at least try. I'm sorry I disobeyed. Guess I'm grounded forever."

"I could have told you that trying to replace Jelly Bean was not a good idea."

"But, Mom…I—"

"I know, Joyce Anne." She folds her arms across her chest. "I know what you wanted. It's not going to work."

I catch Brian out the corner of my eye. He's standing near his truck looking a little scared. A little sad.

"What about Brian? He needs the carburetor."

Mom takes a deep breath through her nose and lets it out slowly.

"I just wanted to do something…something that matters," I say. "Like you help Mrs. Lynch, and Dad fixes everyone's leaks and is on church committees, and Elaine…Elaine's such a good artist and…and—" I sniff back tears and snot. "Bud…well, he's lost now, but he's doing something that matters. I wanted to do something that mattered too. I wanted to help Brian. And at first, that was all I thought until…"

Mom squeezes my shoulder and I say, "Until I left the gate open, and then it became more, I guess. I thought I could replace what I did, like it never happened."

Mom looks into my eyes. She scrutinizes me like she's trying to see clear through my pupils into my heart of hearts. Then she looks at the garage and then back at me. She lets go one of her *I might be sorry for this* sighs. "Come on," she says. "Let's take a look at this flying saucer."

"You really want to see it?"

"Sure, let's see."

Brian flings open the garage door. I see a group of kids led by Beezo and Rat run toward us.

"Quick," Mom says. "Let's get inside and close the door."

I laugh with my mom for the first time since…Jelly Bean died.

Brian turns on that Gustav guy, and the amazing music fills the space.

Mom is looking all around like she's having a hard time finding a focal point or like she's getting swept up in the music and the display. "Impressive," she says.

I smile.

"So you made this?" She looks at Brian. He nods.

"With my Jell-O mold and…and is that my turkey roaster?"

"Uh-huh," I say.

"Oh, good lord, Joyce Anne."

My mother always says, "Oh, good lord, Joyce Anne," when she is upset but also amused at me. It's usually a good sign.

Brian flips on the black light, and my mother kind of swoons when she sees the display in all its grandness.

"How much did you raise?" Mom asks.

Brian flips on the regular lights and turns the music off. "Not enough for a carburetor or a pig," I say.

"This is against my better judgment," Mom says, "but go on and open the show back up. Use the money to help Brian fix his truck. That's a better cause than replacing Jelly Bean right now."

Then she smiles. "You're so much like your father, Joyce Anne. When I think of the crazy things he has built over the years."

"Like your copper pipe lamps?" I say. And I think I might be like her too. With her crocheted-frog toilet-lid cover.

She nods. "Those lamps. Good lord. I'll see you at home. I better go see how your sister is doing, and Joyce…try to forget about the guinea pig."

Forget? How in tarnation am I supposed to forget? She makes

it sound so simple. Like I can just snap my fingers and *Poof!* The memories of Bubba and the gate and Elaine always crying and everyone looking at me with their stern eyes will all just disappear. Like I can just forget that I killed Jelly Bean.

Eighteen

Brian lets out a long, loud whistle. The kind where you don't have to put your fingers in your mouth. The kind of whistle I can never do. He whistles three times, and kids come running.

Linda jumps out from her hiding spot behind Brian's truck. "So, we're back in business?"

"Yep. Get everyone lined up and start collecting money."

She takes a spot near the end of the short driveway. "Line up over here," she says.

Maybe twenty kids, some from the other side of the Park, get in line.

"Word of mouth," I say. "See that? Word of mouth."

Brian smiles. But his smile has a tinge of sadness around the edges. I figure that's because he's both happy and sad. Happy because we might raise enough money and sad because he's getting closer to leaving—and maybe extra sad because of his brother.

"I miss my brother too," I say.

"This is for him too," Brian says. Then he pulls a large piece of cardboard from behind some stacked boxes. Written on it is: *For Mike Hardy.*

Brian gets the Magic Marker and writes: *and Bud.* He looks at me. "What's your last name?"

"Magnin," I said. "Bud *M-A-G-N-I-N.*"

Brian writes my brother's name with large block letters. "I'm gonna hang it on the truck when we ride through the Park in it."

I sniff back even more tears.

He turns on the music. It swirls around the garage and makes me think of faraway places.

Then the exhibit-goers start banging on the garage door.

I swipe away my tears as Brian slides the garage door up a few inches and Kathy DeLuca climbs under for her second chance.

"Wow" is all she says for a second.

"Found right here…at Indian Rock," I say. And then I give the saucer a tiny clandestine nudge and it moves in a circle.

"Cool," Kathy says. "Were there any little green men inside?"

"Nah," Brian says. "It was probably unmanned…on reconnaissance."

I know she doesn't have a clue what *reconnaissance* means.

"OK," I say. "We have to let the next visitor inside."

Kathy ducks under the garage door.

"That was a good one," I say to Brian. "The part about it being on recon—"

"Reconnaissance," Brian says. "That's when a couple of soldiers go out ahead of the others. To check for enemies and..."

"And what?"

"And that's why Mike got clobbered. He was on reconnaissance."

"Wow." I look at my feet because I don't know what else to do.

Donald Crawford slips under the garage door. "So where's this supposed UFO?"

Kids come and go. Some say stuff, some don't. The smaller kids just stand there. I think the music is more unsettling than the UFO. Beezo—who paid twice—tries to mess things up by saying we just used some dumb old Jell-O mold. But Brian stares him down and he backs off.

That's pretty much how it goes until Brian and Linda and I figure no one else is coming.

"So let's count the money," Linda says.

Brian stacks the quarters, while I hold the only dollar bill we have. Linda counts the dimes, nickels, and pennies. "Twelve dollars and ninety-six cents."

"Ninety-six?" Brian said.

"Yeah, well, Francis Xavier DiaMenti only had twenty-one cents," Linda says.

"Not enough," Brian says. "Close, but it's not enough."

I feel kind of like I do when we lose a softball game. But not exactly. This loss feels deeper. Sadder or something.

"Minus my licorice whips," Linda says.

I punch her shoulder. "Shut up about that. I said you'll get your stupid licorice. Sheesh."

"All right already," Linda says. "I was just saying."

"Now what?" Brian asks.

I shrug. "We'll think of something."

"Yeah, right." Brian pushes open the garage door. It jumps the track, which means one of the little wheels somehow comes out of the track. And when that happens, the door is impossible to work. "Now look. Now I gotta fix the dumb garage door."

"That's not so tough. I've seen my dad do it a million times," I say.

Brian scratches behind his neck. He walks over to his truck and lifts the hood. "No carburetor means it's the bus for me and no ride of honor for Mike."

"Or Bud," I say.

"This is too sad," Linda says. "But my mom always says that stuff happens for a reason. Like maybe it ain't such a good idea to drive to Arizona and maybe *you*"—she looks me square in the eye—"ain't supposed to run away because of a guinea pig."

"You don't get it," I say.

"Sure I do. You left the gate open. You gotta live with that whether you're here or in Arizona."

I look at her like she had just that second sprouted broccoli out her ears.

"I better get home," she says. "We have to go to Mass."

Brian and I watch her leave.

"She's right, you know," he says.

I kick one of his truck tires. "I know. But at least in Arizona I won't have to see Elaine's pig nose or that dumb cage with the black ribbons on it."

"Your mom was pretty cool about the whole thing."

"Yeah, I guess, but…but maybe I just don't want to stay here. Because…because of Elaine for one thing, but…what if Bud… dies, like Mike. I don't want to live here anymore."

"That would be rough. But…"

"But I'm still going."

Brian pushes the shoe box into my hands. "You keep the money."

"No. You need a carburetor."

"I'll be taking the bus."

"But what about me? I want to go to Arizona. I just told you."

Brian looks at me. He shrugs. "You can't."

I look at him. Stunned. It is like I am staring at the face of a traitor.

I take off running. Bud taught me to run when I am angry or sad. He said it always helped to run it out. But it doesn't really work this time. When I get home, Elaine is sitting on the stoop like she's waiting for me. It seems as though she's been crying again.

"I was only trying to do something nice," I say. "Even if you don't care."

"How come you didn't check the gate?"

"I already told you. I was in a hurry. And I already told you I was sorry."

She doesn't say anything. So I say, "We didn't raise enough money."

"Too bad," Elaine says. "Now what?"

I shrug. "Guess Brian will take the bus to Arizona." I want to sit next to her and tell her how I was gonna go with him, but now I can't. Instead, I say, "I'll be on the roof."

∽◦∾

I flop into my beach chair. The sun is high and hot, but I don't care. The beach umbrella keeps me in the shade. I look toward

Brian's house, and my chest feels heavy. I grab the binocs and look through them, hoping to see him on the roof. Not yet. I'll wait. I know he'll get there.

I read a little *Alice* while I wait.

Brian never shows up on the roof.

∞

At supper, Dad taps his iced tea glass with his knife and says, "I want you all to know that I have finished the project and will be rolling it out sometime just before dark tomorrow."

That's right. Tomorrow is the Fourth of July. Fireworks. I'd forgotten, what with all the sorrow over Jelly Bean. I love fireworks. I look at Elaine across the table. She is picking apart her meat loaf as usual. She always finds bits of gristle or fat or what she insists are lungs and brain parts in her food. We pretty much ignore her findings.

Anyway, I'm hoping Elaine will smile. But no. Not even fireworks can make her feel better. But at least Dad seems a bit more cheerful. I think working in the garage helps him to not think about Bud and how much he misses him and worries about him.

"So, Dad," I say. "Will you tell us what you built?"

He pulls his fork from his mouth and chews a second or two. "You will all find out tomorrow."

Mom slips Polly a piece of meat loaf. "I saw the flying saucer today. Joyce and that boy, Brian, went on with their UFO display."

Dad glares at me like he just caught me stealing. "You did what?"

"It was for a good cause," I say. "I did it so I could buy Elaine a new pig, but she doesn't want one."

Mom dropped a second helping of meat loaf onto Dad's plate. She often uses food, especially pie, to keep him from blowing his stack. "It was really very good," she says. "Elaine designed it, and Brian built it. I think you'd have liked it."

That gets Elaine talking. "But she had no right to do it without me. It is my flying saucer."

"But I keep telling you I did it for you."

"And I keep telling you I don't want a new guinea pig."

"Well, I can't bring Jelly Bean back from the dead. I would if I could, but I can't. I ain't Jesus Christ."

Polly lets out two sharp barks.

Elaine pushes her chair from the table. "Just shut up, jerk."

"No, you shut up, pig nose," I say.

I drop my fork onto my plate and sip on iced tea to hide the fact that I'm about to cry.

My father slams his fist on the table. "You both stop. This instant."

Elaine runs off from the table and heads for the stairs.

I look at my mom. I want her to say something. Anything that will make this whole mess better.

"She'll get over it, Joyce."

"No she won't. Ever. And neither will I. My life is ruined."

Dad chuckles. "I doubt it."

I dig away at my mashed potatoes and make a small gravy river that swirls around my plate, catching peas along its path like they're small rocks.

"The boy has to move to Arizona," Mom says to Dad.

"Yeah," I say, "because his brother's dead and so is his mom, and his dad can't take care of him anymore."

"It sounds like the poor kid has had his share of trouble."

"I wanted to help him get enough money to buy a carburetor so he could drive his truck and…" I push my plate away and get up from the table. "I ain't hungry anymore. I'll be on the roof."

∽

I am up on the roof not doing anything special except fuming about everything when I hear a noise in our alley. At first, I think it's Dad, but it's Brian. He is pulling a red wagon with the flying saucer in it.

"Joyce," he calls up to me.

"Hey," I say. "What gives?"

He motions for me to climb down.

I move quickly but not too quickly because it is almost dark.

"I brought this back," Brian says when I finally get down to earth. "You should keep it or give it to Elaine or something. Is she around?"

"She's probably in her room." I swallow.

"I decided to let my aunt Natalie buy the bus ticket."

I think for a second or two that Brian is gonna cry. "I'll just leave the truck here. My father said he'd keep it in the back until I graduate from high school and maybe I can fix it then."

The back door opens, and a beam of light shines on Brian's face. His eyes look tired, and he has smudges of grease on his face like he's been working on the truck.

"What's going on?" It's my dad.

"I'm just returning this, sir," Brian says. "Elaine should have it."

Dad moves closer to us and looks at the flying saucer. "So you built this?"

"Yeah. From Elaine's drawing."

Dad snorts a little air out his nose. "Yeah, that girl is somethin'. Draw anything."

"Well, gee," Brian says. "I just wanted to—"

"So Joyce tells me you need a carburetor."

"Yeah, but it looks like I'll never get one."

"I might just have one," Dad says. "What kind of truck?"

"A Ford F-150, 1952," Brian says. His voice rises a little. "But why would you—"

"Used to own one of those beauties," Dad says. "And a few others. Used to work on them all the time. I have some parts in the garage."

Brian just stands there. Dumbfounded or something. It is like he can't find any words, so I say, "Really, Dad? You got one? I mean, you had one all along?"

"Maybe. Let me take a look."

And I thought Mom was the one who kept everything. Now it turns out that Dad is a pack rat too.

He is just about to open the garage door when he says, "I'll go in through the house."

"His secret project is in there," I say. "He is unveiling it tomorrow night, and we're not allowed to see."

Brian and I wait. I am kind of hoping Elaine will come down, and she and Brian will make googly eyes at each other, and maybe things will get back to normal. Romance. I hate romance. But tonight, I'll put up with just about anything if it will help.

"I still want to go with you," I whisper. "If Dad has the carburetor. I can't stay here because, well, you know…because of stuff."

The door opens, and Dad emerges out of the yellow basement light, holding a crumpled box.

"It's all in there," Dad says. "You'll need to rebuild it, clean it real good, but it should work. Even some spare parts."

Brian takes the oily box from Dad. For a second, I think he might cry. He digs around and pulls out a weird, almost square contraption with lots of openings and flaps. He holds it up in the light. "That's it. This will work, sir, thank you. But I can't pay you."

"No need. Now you go on, and be sure to come around tomorrow night just before it gets real dark. I have a surprise."

"You want me to come around?"

Dad puts his hand on his shoulder. "Sure. The whole neighborhood will be out. You're part of the neighborhood, aren't you? Tell your father to come too."

I look at Dad and Brian, and it reminds me of Dad and Bud and how they used to talk to each other and sock each other in the shoulder and make wisecracks. And I know I should feel good for them and even happy for Brian that he got his carburetor. But my insides hurt. I feel sad. Happy and sad at the same time, and it is hard to know which feeling is more important. So I don't choose either one.

Nineteen

That night as I lie on top of the sleeping bag inside my tent, I think about heading out west with Brian. I even say a little prayer that he will get the truck fixed fast and we can leave.

Morning arrives with a shaft of bright sunlight shining into my tent like car headlights. It is the Fourth of July—Independence Day. More importantly, fireworks day.

The ladder is a little slippery from the dew, so I go down carefully.

"Where's Dad?" I ask when I get to the kitchen.

"Basement," Mom says.

I sit at the table. Mom's making French toast. She makes the best. With cinnamon and vanilla. I'm eating mine with butter and sugar this time. Everyone else uses maple syrup.

Mom sets a plate in front of me. "Go on and eat. Elaine will be down soon. I heard her get up a few minutes ago."

"Big deal," I say with a mouthful.

"Don't be that way, Joyce Anne. It takes time."

That's when we hear it. An explosion. Of sorts. Not a big one. But loud.

"What was that?" My fork drops onto my plate. And for an instant, I remember the doorbell and the army officers and the telegram and everyone being sad.

Mom looks stunned for a second too, and then she says, "I'll bet it has something to do whatever your father is doing down there." *BAM!* Another one.

I chew instead of talk and finish my two slices real fast. Mom drops two more onto my plate, and that's when Elaine shows up. She is wearing a tube top and shorts. Mom gives her a scrutinizing look but doesn't say anything. Elaine's hair is tied back in a ponytail. She takes her usual seat and looks across the table at me.

I look away the instant our eyes meet.

"Did you hear that noise?" Elaine asks. "It scared me and—"

"Dad," I say.

Elaine shrugs.

"That boy was here last night," Mom tells Elaine.

"Brian?" Elaine says. And then she gets all dreamy-eyed again. "When? Why didn't anyone tell me?"

"He came to see me," I say, even though that wasn't the whole truth.

"He brought back your flying saucer," Mom says as she sits at the table.

"And Dad gave him a carburetor," I say.

Elaine doesn't say anything right away. She looks at her plate and uses the tip of her fork to swirl melted butter into syrup. "That's nice."

But I know she really doesn't think it's nice. I know she's upset about it because it means Brian is going to head west and she doesn't want him to do that.

"Anyway," Mom says, "don't forget Dad's big surprise this evening. He wants you kids to meet him out back before he unveils the surprise."

"OK," I say. "I can't wait. What is it, Mom?"

Mom shrugs. "Don't know. As long as it's not more lamps, I don't care."

∽

After breakfast, I think a little bit about going over to Brian's. I figure he will be working on the truck. But, nah, I end up hanging out with Linda Costello mostly at her house. We listen to music and play with her stupid Barbie dolls, which I hate, but I do it because my mother told me it is nice to do things your friends want.

I remind her to come by my house for my father's big event—the grand unveiling of whatever he's been building in our garage.

"So what's he got in there?" Linda asks as she pulls a tight-fitting purple dress onto her Barbie.

"Nobody knows, but it's going to be spectacular." I kept tugging on a pink top, trying to get it over Barbie's breasts, but it keeps getting stuck, which makes me think that it's probably a good thing that no real girl has breasts like Barbie's.

"How do you know it's gonna be spectacular? It might be a big, fat bust."

I laugh at the accidental pun Linda has made concerning my Barbie's big bust. "No it won't. You'll see."

We play a little while longer before I tell her that I am still planning to go to Arizona with Brian as soon as he gets the truck running.

She laughs at me.

It hurts my feelings.

"You'll never go," she says. "And besides, it's a lame-brain idea. Your folks will never let you."

"I'm not gonna tell them," I say.

Linda pushes shoes onto her Barbie's feet while I wrestle a looser-fitting yellow blouse onto mine. "Hey," she says. "What about my licorice and my Dots?"

"Oh yeah," I say. I guess I had hoped she'd forgot because my mother took the money and wants me to give it to poor kids, even though Dad says we earned it.

Linda doesn't want to hear any of that.

"I think my mom put the money in the mason jar in the kitchen. My father says we should get it. Split it up between you and me, Elaine and Brian." I grab a piece of paper and do the division.

"That's three dollars and twenty-four cents each."

"But the licorice is coming out of your half."

"Not half. Quarter. And all right. I'll get your licorice."

I shove Barbie into her pink case and close it like a coffin. "Let's go. I'll get the money, and we'll ride up to the candy store." Anything is better than playing with Barbies.

Linda jumps on her bike, which is leaning against the tree in her front yard. She rides slowly while I walk beside her.

When we get to my house, she drops her bike on our sidewalk.

Polly is in the yard. She barks hello.

Linda pats her head. "Wish my parents would let me get a dog."

"Come on," I say. "I'll have to sneak the money."

We tiptoe into the house. Mom is not in the kitchen. The mason jar is on the counter with the money still inside. I twist off the lid and snag a dollar. Plenty for licorice. Then I count out

Linda's share and replace the lid, put the jar back and whisper, "Let's get out of here. I'll tell Mom I owed you. She'll understand."

We tiptoe back outside. I hop on my bike, and off Linda and I ride.

The candy store isn't far. We ride down Oak Avenue and then cut across the Presbyterian church parking lot to the other side where the shortcut dirt road is. We pretty much ride side by side the whole way to the store and drop our bikes right out front. There are a few other bikes there also. The candy store is a pretty neat place. You have to walk down some concrete steps to get into the little shop, which is under a hardware store.

The store is run by Mrs. Walker. We call her the Candy Lady. She has bright-yellow hair and wears bright-red lipstick. She likes to wear cowgirl shirts with rhinestones and sequins and fancy buttons. She always wears jeans and cowgirl boots, although there is nothing in the store that would make you think she had any other interest in cowgirl things, except one picture hanging on the wall of a Palomino horse with a little girl holding the reins. I figure there's a story to be told, lurking behind that picture.

A few kids are ahead of us in line, including Beezo, Rat, and Joey.

"Hey," Beezo says. "Cool UFO. Did it go back to its planet after the show?"

"Yeah," I say. "Didn't you see it last night? It took off around midnight."

"Did not," Rat says.

"Is that what that strange light in the sky was?" the Candy Lady asks, staring straight at me.

"Get outta here," Beezo says. "That was just a fake UFO made from junk."

Linda shrugs. "Think what you want."

Beezo grabs his bag of red dots and caramel swirls.

Rat orders seven Swedish Fish, six caramel swirls, and a pack of Sugar Babies.

Mrs. Walker has all the candy in boxes on three shelves inside a glass case. All you have to do is point to what you want, and she'll drop it into little white bags. Sometimes, she gets a little cranky and yells if we are taking too long.

Joey is just kind of standing there. Then he says to me with a twisted-up face, "Are you for real? Was that a real spaceship?"

"Sure was," I say. "Gone now though." Then I change the subject. "My dad is planning a big surprise tonight for the Fourth of July. Everyone is invited to meet in our alley."

"What kind of surprise?" Rat asks.

"Don't know," Linda says. "Just have to come and see."

"Hey, maybe it's another flying saucer," Beezo says.

I ignore him and ordered Linda's ten red licorice whips.

"And a box of Dots," Linda says.

"And a box of Dots." I roll my eyes.

Mrs. Walker wraps the long, thin whips around her hand to make them more manageable and then pushes them into the bag.

Linda grabs them.

I ask Mrs. Walker for ten caramel swirls. She drops them into a bag, and then I pay for the candy.

"You buying for both of you today, Joyce?" Mrs. Walker asks.

"Yes. It was part of a deal."

"You and your schemes," Mrs. Walker says.

Linda and I jump on our bikes and pedal for home.

"You can have my book collection," I say.

"That's stupid. You ain't going."

"I am too. I'll find a way." I hit a small rock, and my front wheel wobbles. "You'll see. Just do me a favor and tell Elaine that I really am sorry."

"She knows it."

"Then how come she's acting so mean?"

"'Cause it's hard to get over things. Like when you broke the door on my Easy-Bake. Remember?"

I smile. "Yeah. You were pretty sore at me. But it was an accident."

"I know. But I was really mad. But then I got to be OK with it. My door was still busted, but we were still friends. Jelly Bean is still dead, but you and Elaine are still sisters."

Without any pockets, I have to hold the candy bag and the handlebars at the same time, and I can feel the bag getting wet from my sweaty palms. I hate sweaty palms. "She won't ever get over it."

And neither will I.

But I have to try.

I ride ahead of Linda. I pedal harder when we hit the hill. It is so much easier going down the hill. I let go of the handlebars and stretch my arms out and soar. I'm a bird.

Twenty

Finally, after waiting all day, the time comes for the grand unveiling of my dad's latest invention. Even Elaine can't resist. She joins the rest of us—practically the entire neighborhood. Well, our whole block anyway. We are all waiting in the alley for my father to come out of the garage with...well, with whatever he's been hiding. It's pretty exciting. I can feel it in the air. Folks are used to my father doing crazy things, but still...you never know what to expect.

Linda's parents are there. Mrs. Costello is wearing a red-and-white-striped shirt and blue shorts. She looks like an American flag. She and Linda's dad are standing next to Joey Patrillo's parents. Linda is hanging out near me. Her mom obviously forced her to dress for the Fourth—red-and-white-striped shirt, blue shorts, white sneakers. Sheesh.

The DeLucas are there—all nine of them—seven kids and two parents. Even Cass Duthart is standing near her fence. The big, old sourpuss bellyacher. Even she finds it hard to stay away. All in all, I'd say it is a good crowd, prepared for pretty much anything.

Elaine stands off to the side, a little faraway from the main crowd. I don't dare bother her—talk about a sourpuss.

Brian is walking down the alley. He spies Elaine and heads straight for her like he's steel and she's a magnet. They stand kind of close. I can't bear to watch.

The sun is pretty much down. Venus blinks into place as the sky turns grayish-purple with streaks of clouds, the color of my mother's silvery pie tins. It is almost time to head to Clifton Field for the fireworks display. My father better not make us miss it. Some of the other people in the crowd are getting restless.

"Come on, Magnin," calls Nick DeLuca Senior. "We gotta get to the field."

"Yeah," Mrs. Costello says. "We want to see what you got cooking."

Then it happens. The garage door opens a couple of inches, and then *BAM*, Dad pushes it open the whole way. It slams against the ceiling and rattles the tracks.

"Happy Fourth of July," Dad says.

I crane my neck to try to see what he has been hiding. But all I see is a strange mound, something covered by a large canvas tarp. That has to be it—for sure. I glance at Elaine and Brian. She is actually smiling, and I figure that's a good thing. Even if it is because of Brian and his googly eyes.

Dad pushes the contraption onto the driveway pad.

"Ladies and gentleman," he says. "Boys and girls. In honor of this day of independence and in the hope that our sons and brothers, our daughters and sisters will all come home soon." He looks at Brian. "And in honor of those who won't be back. I present—"

A fanfare of trumpets blares from our house. Mom is standing at the dining room window. She must be working the portable CD player. Dad rigged up some speakers so they'd blast out loud.

"It gives me great honor to present the Cannon of Freedom and Liberty." Dad looks so proud with his chest puffed out and a smile as wide as all outdoors. It is nice to see him smile—really smile.

He snaps off the canvas, and lo and behold, there it is. A cannon!

An actual cannon with a long, copper barrel with a diameter about the size of the large Skippy jar. The whole thing is on wagon wheels. My father has built a cannon.

I lean in to Linda. "Now that's cool."

No one else moves or does anything. Then slowly, clap by clap, the crowd applauds and cheers.

"Does it work?" hollers Nick DeLuca Senior.

"It sure does," Dad says.

"Is that thing even legal?" calls Mr. Costello.

Dad doesn't answer him. "Follow me," he says instead.

Dad pulls the cannon on a rope like it's a kids' pull toy and heads down the alley. The whole crowd follows behind. We all light our punks, which are sticks made of bamboo and coated with horse manure or sometimes sawdust. Dad likes to say they're all horse manure because it makes people screw up their faces and say, "Ewwwww." Anyway, in the dark, the punks are like fireflies, and we follow Dad down to Scullion Field. Linda says he's the Pied Piper. I smile and glance over at Elaine. She has her punk, and she's walking with Brian. Dad pulls the cannon through the gate and out into the center of the field, right onto the pitcher's mound.

"Sit on the bleachers," Dad says in a loud voice. "Sit on the bleachers. Don't want anyone to get hurt."

"He's not going to fire that thing," Mr. Hazel says.

"I hope not," Nick Deluca Senior's wife, Ann, says. "But he just might. He's a nut."

"Sure, he's going to fire it," says Nick. "And he ain't a nut. The man's a genius."

I guess in a way, my dad is a genius—the way he can build the things he imagines. And he might be a nutjob too. I know that he is going to blast that cannon into the night. I wonder if it's his way of trying to send a signal to Bud. Like somehow the blast will make it all the way to wherever my brother is, and he'll hear it and say, "That's my dad."

Elaine and Brian sit next to each other on a top row. Real close. Their knees touch. I wonder if she knows he's leaving soon. I wonder if he'll tell her I'm planning on going to Arizona with him.

The next thing I know, my mother is standing on the pitcher's mound with my father. She raises her hands to quiet everyone, and then she bursts into song.

"O beautiful for spacious skies, for amber waves of grain…"

Pretty soon, the whole crowd is singing along with my mom.

After the song, Dad pulls a box of stick matches from his pants pocket. "Now this should work. I couldn't really give it a proper test but here goes."

A gasp filters through the crowd. The cannon is, of course, pointed away from the bleachers. The barrel is nearly raised to point straight up toward the moon.

Dad lights a long fuse. He grabs my mom's hand, and they run for dear life toward the bleachers.

And then…

KA-BLAM!

The sky lights up with the prettiest firework colors—red and blue and yellow. And then another one. *KA-BLAM!* More colors rain down. Red in the shape of an umbrella.

Then Dad runs out and shoves something in the barrel and lights it again. And again. And again.

About ten minutes later, Dad runs out of fireworks, and my mother starts singing again, this time "The Star-Spangled Banner." Which she doesn't do very well. Happy Fourth of July.

Mom hugs Dad. I think he's crying a little because he wipes his eyes.

"That's it," Dad says. "That's the show." Smoke still pours out of the cannon barrel. And I am so proud of my dad.

The crowd applauds as Dad takes a graceful bow. The bleachers clear quickly as folks make their way to Clifton Field through the lingering gray smoke for the real fireworks display.

"Wow, Dad," I say. "Where did you get fireworks?"

"Customer paid me in fireworks for installing a water heater."

Good old Dad. He often gets paid in cookies and fudge, but this is the first time he's gotten paid in fireworks.

Dad puts his arm around Mom. "Should we go to Clifton?"

She shakes her head. "This was enough for one night. Let's just go home."

I give a quick look around. I don't see Elaine or Brian.

"You go ahead to the field, Joyce," Dad says. "Just don't stay out too late."

"OK," I grab Linda Costello's hand, and we run toward Clifton.

"My father says your dad is crazy," Linda says.

"Yep. He sure is."

Twenty-One

A few days after the big Fourth of July extravaganza, I go to my bedroom—the one inside the house—and make a discovery. Jelly Bean's cage is missing. There's just a picture of her in a silver frame sitting on the table where her cage used to be. It makes me stop dead in my tracks.

"Where's the cage?" I ask Elaine, who is drawing as usual.

"Basement," is all she says.

"What are you drawing?"

"None of your business."

I try to sneak a peek. I'm pretty sure she's drawing Brian.

I pull a pair of shorts from a drawer. My blue shorts with the red Italian ice stain from when Elaine and I went to Rosatti's and got Italian ice, and my paper cone had a rip and the cherry ice leaked out. For a second, it makes me think about how much I miss my sister and wish she would come back to me. Then maybe I could change my mind about Arizona.

"I might go to Brian's house today," I say as I slip the shorts on. "He might be finished fixing the truck. Wanna come?"

"No."

"He might be getting ready to drive it around the Park and then to Arizona."

"I don't care."

But I think she does care.

I swallow twice because I'm thinking about telling Elaine that I plan to go with him. I guess I'm staring at her because she says, "Take a picture. It will last longer."

"Just thinking," I say. "Maybe I'll go with Brian to Arizona. How would you like *that*?"

Elaine laughs a little. "You're crazy. Dad will never let you."

"Maybe I won't tell him."

And I sashay out the door. That's what Mom would say I did. *Sashay*. It means to walk casually, like you just don't care what people think, but you use exaggerated movements with your hips and shoulders. It's kind of uppity.

∽

Polly and I run over to Crestview. Brian is out back as usual, working on the truck. Only this time, the truck is running. It's kind of sputtering, but still, it's the first time I've heard the truck run. It must be music to Brian's ears. I also hear the flying saucer music coming from the garage, and it makes me feel…something. I'm not sure what exactly, but the closest I can explain is to say that the music makes me feel homesick. I figure Brian must really like it.

"You got it working," I say. "That's terrific."

"Yeah, sorry I haven't been around much…you know, up on the roof and stuff. I've been pretty busy."

Brian doesn't sound excited. Instead, he sounds like the music makes me feel: homesick.

"It took a few days to rebuild that carburetor. But it works great now," he says.

"So I guess you'll be getting ready to drive it to Arizona."

"Yeah, s'pose so." He looks at me like he wants to say something else, but he changes his mind and says, "Elaine doing better? You know, with…everything."

"She's just drawing as usual, and I'm not sure if she's doing better. I think my dad took Jelly Bean's cage away."

"That's good," Brian says. "Good to get rid of reminders, except…my dad still has some of Mom's clothes hanging around and…"

He rubs the truck fender.

"And you have Mike's truck," I say. "Guess it's hard to get rid of the things that matter."

"Yeah." Brian looks into the engine. "Yeah, sure is."

"So when are we leaving?" I ask.

"We?" Brian says. "You still want to come with me? You sure?"

"Yeah."

Polly lets out a loud bark.

"I thought you might change your mind on account of…" He looks at me. "Never mind."

"So when?" I ask. "So I can plan."

"Tomorrow is the tenth. I'll drive her around the Park. You know, for Mike's birthday." He taps on something in the engine. "And for Bud."

My stomach goes wobbly. "I'm ready." But I can feel my face turn red from my neck to my cheeks. I blush like that when I'm scared or nervous, and in that moment, I am both.

"How far is it to Arizona?" I ask.

"Two thousand, three hundred and forty miles…give or take. I figured it out on the map."

Wow. Two thousand, three hundred and forty miles. I gulp air. That's far. I'd never been any farther away from home than Charleston, South Carolina.

I watch him fiddle with a few things under the hood. "Dad says he's got the gas money, but it's not too late to go by bus…if I want."

"Guess I'll be over tomorrow," I say.

∞

I head straight back to my house, with Polly close to my knees. She knows when something is up, and I have the distinct impression she does not want me to go—but I have to. I have to leave now. I don't think I can live another day in the same house with Elaine when she won't forgive me. When things will never, ever be the same.

The first thing I do is find my mother. She is working with her African violets. She pulls dead leaves from them, only they aren't always completely dead. Mom has a way of sitting the leaf in a shallow glass of water, and in a few days, the leaf grows roots.

"Mom," I say. "I was just wondering something."

"What's that?" she says without looking at me.

"I was…I was wondering when the army will find Bud."

She stops her work and looks out the window like she's looking clear to Vietnam. She takes a breath and says, "I don't know, Joyce. All we can do is hope it will be soon."

"But they'll find him, right, Mom? They'll find him."

Mom puts her hand on my cheek. "Sure. Sure they will."

"OK. I was just checking."

"You should have lunch," Mom says.

I pour myself a glass of iced tea. "Is Elaine better now?"

"For the most part. Letting Dad take the cage was a big thing. She'll be fine soon."

After eating my peanut butter sandwich, I go to my room upstairs. Elaine isn't there. Maybe she went over to Sac's. Her sketchbook is on her bed. I am forbidden from ever opening her sketchbook.

I sit on her bed and open the large tablet. The first page has pictures of Jelly Bean. The page after that has pictures of eyes and flying saucers. And then there is a page of Brians. She drew him really well. I knew right away it was him. And there is a page of Buds and more Jelly Beans.

Then I find a page of me. Me and the side-yard gate. It makes my stomach hurt. I find a pencil on the table and I write across the page. "I said I was SORRY." And then I add seven exclamation points.

I leave the sketchbook and head for the roof. I'll just wait there until tomorrow. Until Brian is ready to go.

Twenty-Two

The next morning, I pack some clothes in a brown paper bag. Just extra shorts and socks, underpants, and two shirts, both striped. I don't need anything else, except my binoculars. You can never tell when they'll come in handy. I also grab my toothbrush and a comb. My hair gets snarly in the car with the windows down.

Mom is in the kitchen making Dad's breakfast. He's at the table reading his paper.

I sneak past them. I pat Polly on the head. She lets out a bark. "Shhh," I say. And then I slip out the front door and up the ladder to the roof, where I grab my binoculars. I take in the view because it's probably the last time I'll see the world from here. Then it's down the ladder to earth, where I touch the peach tree. I can smell the sap. It's sweet and oily, and I stand for just a moment on the spot—the spot where Jelly Bean died and now she's buried. I grab hold of one of the ripening peaches and yank it from the branch. I toss it hard against the house. No peach ice cream for me this year.

But just before I get totally filled with tears, I run. When I get to the end of our sidewalk, I stop and look back. A tear rolls down my cheek, and I swallow hard. I see Polly at the window. She has her paws resting on the sill.

∞

Brian is in his garage. He is just closing the record player. "I think I'll bring Mom's records."

Then he looks at me standing there holding my brown bag. "Whatcha got in the bag?"

"My stuff, silly. Clothes and my toothbrush."

"Oh, I… Ugh." He shakes his head and says, "I don't think you're gonna like what I gotta say."

I look him square in the eye. "What? Say what?"

Brian looks away for a second and then says, "I can' take you. I-I never thought you were dead serious anyway."

I think maybe my heart stops beating for a second or two, and I feel a rush of red flood my face like it always does when I'm nervous or upset.

"But I am serious. I'm ready to go. I told you. I can't stay here anymore."

Brian takes a breath. "Well, you can't blame me. I—"

"Blame you? For what?"

"For making you think it was OK for you to come. I can't take you. Holy cow. You're just a kid."

I look at my sneakers. "Oh. Just a kid. A kid who kills guinea pigs and puts on fake UFO shows and…and tries to make everybody forgive her when they don't want to and…a kid who doesn't have anything—"

"What do you mean? You got stuff."

"I don't mean stuff. I mean…I mean a reason for—"

Brian pulls himself up to his full height and looks down at me, and that's the first time I see how much taller he is than me. Taller and older and bigger than me. He's right. I'm just a kid. A kid with no reason except to play ball and read books and wonder about things like missing brothers and why sisters can't say "It's OK" when you mess up. That's all I want. A brother who ain't lost and a sister who says "It's OK."

"You got reasons to stay," Brian says. "You have Elaine and your dad and your mom. And a brother who ain't dead."

"Yeah. Right," I say. I choke on tears. I have absolutely no interest in letting them pour out of my eyes in front of him.

"But look," Brian says, "I still want you to ride with me around the Park—just like we planned. If it wasn't for you, I'd never have gotten the carburetor, and I'd be heading to the bus station now."

"I guess," I say.

"And I got to tell you something else. Dad's coming with me. Help me drive and stuff. Then he'll fly back." He puts the record player into the back of the truck. "Dad had to go into work for a little while. We're heading out as soon as he gets back."

So there's no way I can go. His dad won't let me.

We climb into the truck. The seat is pretty torn up, and it isn't at all comfortable. Brian turns the key, and the truck starts right up. He smiles so hard I think he might bust.

I smile too. Even if I don't get to go to Arizona, I can't help but feel good about the truck running. I got to help Brian with something important. If he'd never met me, he wouldn't have gotten the carburetor. And helping him get his brother's truck running feels as important as sewing for women who have been burned or letting poor customers pay with fireworks instead of money.

Brian reaches into his shirt pocket and pulls out a picture of a boy wearing a Phillies baseball cap and smile just like Brian's. He looks at it for a second and then puts it on the dashboard right behind the steering wheel. "This ride's for you, Mikey."

Then next thing I know, we're cruising down Crestview.

"I told you I'd get her runnin'," Brian says.

"I know," I say. But then I figure out he's talking to Mike.

We drive down Oak Avenue, Palmer Mill, Westbrook Drive.

It's not like people line the streets like when the Memorial Day parade passes by, but the mailman waves and Mrs. Wilbur stops for a second and stares. We drive onto my street.

"This part's for Bud," Brian says.

I look at my house, the peach tree, the patio, and the front door. I look up at the roof.

"Thanks, Brian," I say. "For Bud."

We head toward Scullion Field. We get almost to the end of the block when I hear something. Someone is hollering, "*Stop! Stop!*"

Brian looks in the rearview. "It's Elaine."

I look behind me, but I can't see much through the tiny truck window.

Brian pulls along the curb.

Elaine catches up with us. She runs around to my side. She still thinks I'm going to Arizona. Maybe she doesn't want me to go. Maybe she's ready to say, "It's OK."

"Look," she says, waving a small piece of yellow paper. "It's a telegram. From the army. They found him. He's OK. He's in the hospital."

"Your brother?" Brian asks.

"He's gonna come home," Elaine says. "Dad's been looking all over for you."

I look at Brian.

"That's great," he says. "Wow. Really great." He reaches over me and pushes open the passenger door. "Hop in."

Elaine climbs over me and sits between me and Brian. "He's coming home."

I feel my eyes well up with tears. Elaine looks like she already cried a bucket.

Brian honks the horn and hollers. "He's coming home."

We drive down a few more streets honking the horn and hollering, "He's coming home. He's coming home. Bud is coming home."

I glance at Elaine and think how good it is to see her smile.

A few doors open and people step out onto their stoops to see what the commotion is about.

"Bud Magnin is coming home," I holler. "The army found my brother."

Brian drives a victory lap around the Park, then he takes us back to our house.

"Thanks," I say with my hand on the door handle. But now I have to say good-bye to Brian. I wonder how to do it because my feelings are kind of jumbled around. I'm happy that Bud is coming home but sad that Brian is leaving and still unsure of Elaine and how she feels about me. "Have a good trip to Arizona." It's all I can think to say until I blurt out, "Thanks for helping with the flying saucer."

Brian nods at me.

"Do you have to go?" Elaine asks.

"Maybe I'll come back after next school year." He smiles real wide. "People come back."

Elaine and I stand in the street. I sneak closer to her and grab her hand. She doesn't let go or push me away. We watch Brian drive out of sight.

"It's gonna be OK," I say.

Twenty-Three

Everything isn't OK.

We get word that something went south, as Dad says, and Bud needs surgery now. It's the worst news ever.

Elaine goes right back to not talking to me unless she absolutely has too. It's like standing in the street holding my hand never happened. She sees more flying saucers and continues to draw pictures of Jelly Bean and Brian and to paint flowers and peace signs.

Mostly, things feel weird. Mom cooks and hums and picks aphids off her African violets. Dad goes to work every day, and I stay on the roof.

Finally, on a hot night in August when I'm just done washing the dishes, Bud calls. He calls during Walter Cronkite. He only talks to Dad.

"Two days. Thursday," Dad says when he hangs up the phone. "He's coming home in two days. We'll pick him up at the Greyhound station." He puts his arm around Mom and lets out a huge breath—a breath he's been holding for months. He kisses Mom's cheek, and she wipes her eyes on her apron. "Two days." She holds her fingers up. "Two."

∽

Then it's Thursday, and we all drive into Philadelphia to pick up Bud. He's coming in on a Greyhound bus from Fort Dix, New Jersey, because that's where they sent him after a hospital stay in Germany. I guess we'll learn more about that later. Dad says he would have driven to New Jersey to get him, but Bud told him the army had to do it their way.

It's raining cats and dogs on the way to the bus station. Dad has the wipers going a mile a minute, and Mom is real quiet, like if she talks, she'll cry because of how happy she is that Bud is coming home. She has a whole big party planned for him and everything.

Bolts of lightning and rumbles of thunder startle me. But I keep my eyes peeled for the station. I look through my binocs, hoping I'll be the first to see him. I know Polly is gonna go crazy when she sees him. We left her sitting by the front door waiting. She knows all right. She knows Bud is coming home.

"There's the station," Dad says. "It's hard to see in this rain, and I don't see any spots. I…guess we'll park around the corner."

I look through my binocs. The light at the station is eerie.

Yellow with neon signs that read *Bus Station*, with an arrow pointing down creepy, dark steps.

Lots of boys in uniforms are standing around outside the rectangular building, probably waiting for cars full of families to pick them up. I keep looking and looking while Dad searches for a spot. I see so many faces, and in a weird, eerie kind of way, they all look the same. Tired. Anxious. I keep looking. I want to be the first to spot him. I don't know why. I just do. I figure it will be one of those things I'll never, ever forget. The day I saw my brother who we thought might die come home from war.

Then, all of a sudden, like one of those pictures that when you stare at it long enough a new picture materializes, I see him. And for like three seconds, his is the only face I see. I want him to see me too. I want us to lock eyes and smile at the same time. But no, he doesn't see me. Not yet.

"I see him," I say. "He's standing over there. By the Coke machine."

"Where?" Mom says.

"Right there." I point.

Dad pulls closer and rolls down his window, even though the rain is streaming in like gangbusters. "Bud," he calls. "Buddy."

"He's coming," I say. "He's walking this way." He's kind of limping. Walking slow.

"Let him in," Dad says. "Open the door."

Elaine pushes open her door, but Mom has already opened her door and jumped out of the car. Another car beeps. But we don't care. Mom runs around the front of the car. She reaches out for Bud and they hug. She kisses his cheeks and hugs him again.

Bud pushes his green duffel bag into the car. He climbs into the backseat. Elaine gives him a big hug. I want to hug him too, but I can't with Elaine in the way. But Bud reaches out, and we touch hands for a second. I can't think of a single thing to say. All I can do is cry, but I turn my face to the window so no one will know.

∞

When we get home, Dad shakes Bud's hand about a dozen times until he finally hugs him. "So glad you're home, Son."

Boy, is Polly glad to see Bud. She barks and dances, and when he sits down, she climbs right into his lap—which is kind of funny because Polly is pretty big—and licks his face about a million times. "Good old girl," Bud says. "I missed you too."

Mom makes Bud a cup of tea. He's always liked tea. Earlier in the day, she also made fudge—his favorite. Tea and fudge.

I sit on the other side of the living room in the blue chair. Elaine sits near Bud on our green couch. I want to jump into his lap like Polly. But that will not be a good idea. I have to consider the surgery he had. I figure I will wait a while and then talk to him when he's used to being home more. I want to know where he was when the army couldn't find him. He looks different. His face isn't quite as chubby. He is wearing strange black-rimmed glasses, and his hair is so short, I can hardly see it. His army uniform looks baggy on him, and I think his army hat is funny looking.

He notices me looking at him. "So what's up, Shortstop?"

"Nothin'," I say, glad to be called Shortstop again.

Bud yawns and drinks tea and eats fudge while everyone fusses. But no one asks him about the war or about what he did.

Mom tells him about the coming-home party, but Bud only smiles.

"So pretty much everyone will be at the party tomorrow," Mom says. "Mrs. Tomlinson is making her famous lasagna." She sounds nervous, and then all of a sudden, everyone seems nervous. Even Dad doesn't know what to do with his hands. And I wonder if all the families with sons or daughters returning from war feel the same way. We're supposed to be happy, and we are, but everything is different somehow and I can't explain it. If feelings were colors and happy was bright purple, then my family is blue-gray, the color in the crayon box no one uses, except for rain clouds.

"Joyce killed Jelly Bean," Elaine blurts out all of a sudden without anyone asking her.

"She didn't mean to," Mom says. "It was an accident."

Bud looks at me. "For real? That's too bad."

"We'll have none of this tonight," Dad says. "Bud's home. And we're done talking about the pig."

Bud pushes Polly off his lap. "I'm kinda tired. Think I'll hit the sack."

"Good idea," Dad says. "We'll have plenty of time to catch up. Maybe we can do some fishing or toss the baseball tomorrow."

"Maybe," Bud says. He grabs his duffel bag.

We all watch him go upstairs like he's done a gazillion times before. But it's different this time. He walks slowly, as though he wants to feel every step beneath his feet—just to be sure. Just to be certain he's home and he's A-OK. Everything is back to normal, but nothing is the same.

Twenty-Four

Dad makes me sleep in the bedroom because of the storm and because of Bud. "I want my entire family *under* one roof," Dad says.

It's OK. I want to sleep in my bed and be closer to Bud. We all go to bed early that night. Even Mom, and she always stays up to watch the eleven o'clock news.

"Why'd you tell him about Jelly Bean?" I ask Elaine as I slip out of my shorts. I decide to sleep in just a shirt and underpants. It is really hot and steamy after the rain.

"Because it's true."

∽

The next morning, Mom goes to Ninth Street to do some last-minute party shopping. Dad stays home from work to help get the house ready. Even Elaine pitches in. She makes pretty paper flowers using colored tissue paper and pipe cleaners. She runs streamers from each corner of the living room to the middle. It's a little like being under a circus tent.

Bud stays in his room all day. I keep walking past, hoping he'll open his door or come out and talk to me. I plan to ask him to toss a ball around or maybe show him my camp on the roof. Polly stays right by his door nearly the whole day. She only goes outside to pee. I hear her whimper a couple of times, and it makes me angry and sad that Bud won't open the door and let her in. How come he doesn't even want to talk to Polly?

"When will Bud get up?" I ask my dad as he dusts the stereo.

"He's tired. Let him sleep."

"But I don't think he is sleeping," I say. "I think he's up and just won't come out."

"That's OK too. It takes time to adjust. He's been gone a long time. Maybe I should bring him something to eat," Dad says.

"Can I bring it to him?"

Dad tosses me the dusting cloth and the Pledge. "You dust. I'll make him a sandwich."

∞

Around six thirty, people start coming to our house for the party. Nearly everyone from the neighborhood shows up and a lot of people from church. Mr. Marsden is wearing his World War II army uniform. Mom says he looks proud as a peacock and wants to show off his medals to Bud. Nearly everyone has a gift for Bud, and most bring food—lots and lots of food, including Mrs. Costello's Lime Jell-O surprise with bits of carrots in it. It looks sickening.

Mom has chairs set up around the living room and the dining room. Dad puts the Serendipity Singers on the stereo. They are Bud's favorites, even though they're a pretty ancient group. I like them too, especially the song about putting beans in your ears. It isn't until the music starts that Bud comes downstairs. He's not wearing his uniform. He's wearing brown pants and a short-sleeved brown shirt with little yellow trout all over it.

"And here's our guest of honor," Mom says. She puts her arm through his and leads him to the big chair. The one Dad always sits in to watch the news.

Everyone applauds, just like Dad wanted, because Bud's a hero.

I think Bud is only pretending to be happy and glad to see everyone. He let Mrs. Tomlinson kiss his cheek and Bill Rankin tussle his hair—what little he had—because he is polite. I know he wants to be just about anywhere but in our living room pretending to be happy and pretending to like all the gifts. He got a pen and pencil set, three new shirts, and cologne. But the biggest gift, the one from my parents, is a tape-recording deck. It is huge, with big reels and fancy dials and a microphone. Bud likes that gift for real.

He likes sound and music, and he records trains and car horns just for fun.

"That's the best on the market," Dad says. "Top of the line."

Bud smiles. "Thanks, Pop. It's terrific."

"Record us," Mrs. Tomlinson says with a chuckle in her voice. "Go on, Buddy, record the party."

"Maybe we could sing," Mom says.

But Bud shoves the tape recorder back into the box. "Not right now. I have to learn how to use it first."

That's a lie. Bud could figure that thing out in two shakes of lamb's tail. He just doesn't want to play along.

Then, all of a sudden, Phil Franklin pipes up. He is one of the church deacons who sells insurance the rest of the week and is a total pain in the ass. At least that's what my dad says. Anyway, Phil Franklin goes, "So Mavis Stearn told me her cousin Kevin got both his legs blown off over there. His truck ran over mines. Said a little kid got killed when it happened."

Bud's eyes get wide, while nearly everyone else in the room gasps like a grizzly bear just walked into the room.

"What's wrong?" Mr. Franklin says. "What did I say?"

"Hush now," Mrs. Lynch says. "None of them boys can be held responsible if civilians die. It's the government over there using them poor, innocent kids as human shields."

Bud puts his iced tea glass on the coffee table. "Excuse me. I just need to get some air."

"You go right ahead, Son," Mom says. "I'll get the cake ready." Then she glares daggers at Mrs. Lynch.

The crowd parts like the Red Sea as Bud limps to the front door. He crunches the wrapping paper he dropped on the floor. I follow him, even though Dad catches hold of my shirt. "You stay put."

I yank it away. "No."

∽

Bud is standing near my ladder.

"What's this for? Dad doing some work?"

"I moved to the roof on account of Jelly Bean, Elaine and her stupid flying saucers, and everyone being so sad after the army lost you."

"Elaine's still seeing things?" He just ignores the last part.

"Yeah. She sees flying saucers mostly. And eyes."

"Not much of a reason to move to the roof."

"I probably would move back now that you're home, but…" I look at him. He still looks tired. "But what?" he asks.

"But she hates me on account of the pig."

Bud nods. "Whatcha got up there?"

"Want to see?"

Bud climbs the ladder. I follow, and he helps me over the ridge, even though I don't need any help. I take it anyway. It's good to have him home.

"Nice. You got everything you need."

"Snacks, books, binoculars," I say.

"But only one chair," he says. "I call dibs." He plunks himself into it.

I upend my bucket of snacks and sit near him.

"Lots of stars," he says, looking at the night sky, which is draped down around us. "It's really clear now, washed fresh from the rain."

"You ever gonna tell us how you got lost?"

Bud opens my bag of chips and eats a few. "Don't think so."

"That's OK. It's like the pig, I guess. I got real sick of talking about it and saying I was sorry."

"It was an accident," Bud says. "Right?"

"Not really. I didn't check the gate like we're supposed to. I heard Jelly Bean squeal, and I ran back and saw Bubba—"

"That's all right. I get the picture. You didn't check twice, and Bubba got the pig."

"Yeah. I left the gate open."

"Yeah, I made mistakes too. Over there."

I grab the binocs and look at the moon. Waiting.

"I guess we both feel sorry for stuff," he says finally. He takes the binoculars from me. "Ever see the man in the moon?"

"Nah, I keep looking, but I just don't get it."

"Me neither. I just don't get it." He bumps his shoulder against mine. "If it helps, I forgive you." He hands me back the binoculars.

"Yeah. Same for you. Even if you did make mistakes, that doesn't mean you're not my brother anymore. Doesn't mean I don't love you."

He love-punches my shoulder. "Same goes for you. I think Elaine still loves you too."

"Maybe." I look through the binocs. "Maybe we'll see a flying saucer tonight."

He laughs a little. "Just stop teasing her about it. She'll stop seeing them some day."

"I guess."

That's when we hear the ladder rattle against the house. I rush to the side. "It's Elaine. She's never been up here. You better help her."

"Easy," Bud says. "One rung at a time. Go slow. I'll help you over the ridge."

I hear Elaine say, "Stupid tree."

Then she's on the roof. She looks out of place, standing there looking at my camp. She doesn't say anything at first. It's like she's trying to get her bearings.

"So what brings you up here?" Bud asks.

"Dad. He asked me to find you. The guests are wondering what happened."

"Yeah. We better get back to the party."

Bud looks at me. "You sleeping up here tonight?"

I shake my head. "Nah. I think I want to come back inside."

Elaine looks me square in the eyes, and for a second, I think I might fall off the roof when she says, "Yeah. School starts soon. You better come inside."

"OK," I say. "Mom will probably make me now anyway."

"Cool," Elaine says. "Cool." Then I think I'm gonna cry, but I don't because of the party and because of Bud.

∞

The next day, Dad hauls a basket of peaches into the kitchen.

"They ripe?" Mom asks.

"Just ripe enough for ice cream," Dad says.

I'm sitting at the table eating a tuna sandwich. "Really, Dad? Ice cream?"

He tussles my hair. "Yep. I'm gonna go get rock salt, and we'll make ice cream after your mother finishes peeling and slicing."

I look at Mom. She just smiles and says, "I'll get my knife. Joycie, you can help."

After I help peel about nine peaches, I look at Mom and say, "Remember the day we got the telegram. The first one?"

She nods but doesn't say anything.

"I went outside that day and the peach tree was just starting to get her peaches. The flowers were pink and white, and I stood there and watched and then one of the buds broke off the stem and tumbled to the ground. I saw it. It was like super slow-motion. And it made me worry."

Mom drops more sliced peaches into a bowl. "Why?"

"I was afraid it meant Bud was dead. It felt like everything might die. I thought there'd be no peaches or anything else that is good. Ever again."

"But Bud is here," she says. "Home safe and sound. And here are the peaches. The only way for the peaches to grow is *if* the buds fall off. It's nature's way. Some things need to die before other things can grow."

At first, that doesn't make sense. I think about Brian's brother dying. And I think about Jelly Bean. What is growing in their places? Elaine hating me? Sadness? Nothing sweet like peaches. I think about Bud too, even though he didn't die like Brian's brother, not completely anyway, but he is definitely not the same Bud.

∽

A couple of days later, I ride my bike down the alley behind Brian's house just to see if maybe he changed his mind and came back. No, his house looks like no one lives there anymore.

When I get to the end of the block, I see Beezo standing in the alley. He's holding a sign, and I remember Brian and his sign. I think of all that happened because I moved to the roof and read Brian's sign.

But even so, I stop to read Beezo's sign. It says, *Kittens. $1.00.* "Whaddja do?" I ask. "Steal them?"

Beezo lets out a noise and says, "Nah, our cat had another litter, and my old man is makin' us get rid of them. Says they all go to the SPCA if we don't find homes for them."

So I drop my bike and go inside Beezo's garage. Rat's there with a basket of kittens. Four of them. Pure white, furry and soft, with huge blue eyes. They meow and try to claw out of the basket, but Rat keeps pushing them back.

"Come on," he says. "You know you can't resist."

My eyes light on the scrawny one in the back. She's nuzzling the basket kind of like Jelly Bean used to nuzzle her cage or Elaine's neck. This kitten is the only one with a patch of brown, the same color as my mother's coffee after she adds cream, the same color as the patches on Jelly Bean's wide middle, the same color as some of the camouflage on Bud's army pants. And that's when I know what's right to do. I reach into my pocket and pull out four quarters from my flying saucer money. "I'll take the scrawny one. Should be only fifty cents, considering how tiny she is."

"You're nuts," Beezo says. "A buck or go home."

I ride home with the kitten in one hand, snuggled up against my neck. I steer with the other. I pull into my front yard, drop my bike, and go racing into the house. I dash upstairs, hoping Elaine is in our room. I stand at the doorway and see her sitting on her bed as usual with her sketchbook.

I tuck the kitten under my shirt.

"Hey," I say. "Whatcha doin'?"

Elaine looks at me for about half a second, but that's better than before when she wouldn't look at me at all.

I reach under my shirt and pull out the kitten. I pry one of her claws from my skin, but I don't care how much it hurts. "Look." I move closer to her bed. The kitten meows and mews. She sounds a little like Jelly Bean, only softer.

I reach the kitten out to Elaine. "She's for you. I know I can't give you Jelly Bean back, but maybe this kitten—"

Elaine doesn't move. She looks back at her book and scribbles, hard.

"She's soft," I say.

I wait for her to at least look at me. Look at the kitten. But she just keeps scribbling.

"Please," I say.

Finally, Elaine looks at me.

I can see in her eyes that she's not sure what to do. And I can almost see a neon sign over her head flashing: *No. It's too soon.*

But the longer I stand there with the kitten trying to get back inside my shirt, the more faint the sign grows until *Poof!* It's gone. I wait for Elaine to make a move. She sets her pencil down.

My heart pounds.

She moves her book to the side.

My heart pounds faster.

"Please? She needs you."

Elaine reaches out. I see her eyes glisten like she's really gonna turn on the waterworks now. I place the kitten in her hands, and she pulls it close to her neck. The kitten mews and nuzzles her.

I feel my toes curl like they do when I'm really scared. When I'm not sure if I'm doing or saying the right thing or I have to stand up in front of the whole class and deliver a book report on a book I didn't finish reading.

"I really am sorry," I say. "I know I'll spend my whole life bein' sorry, but maybe the kitten—"

Elaine looks at me, and I stop talking because I figure I can't say anything else that would make a nickel's worth of difference.

"It's OK," she says. But she doesn't say it in the way that makes me feel like I've just been brushed aside. I take a deep, shaky breath and let it go.

"She's really soft and warm and…and…and listen… She's purring," I say.

I move closer. Slow. But then I sit next to Elaine, and she all of a sudden pulls me in to her. I hear the kitten purr between us, and I know it really is OK or at least it's gonna be OK.

And that's good enough for me. I'll live with "It's OK."

Acknowledgments

Stories rarely come fully formed. They take a lot of hard work and digging to become complete. This was certainly true for *Jelly Bean Summer*. I knew I wanted to write about this true event from my childhood, but it took the wise counsel of many people to get it just right. First, I need to say think you to the folks at Highlights Writers Workshops who helped me shape and get to the core of the story: the great and wonderful Patti Lee Gauch and the amazing Kathy Erskine. I also need to thank my dear friend Pam Halter who reads every word I ever write before anyone else. My beloved CRUE—an incredible assortment of friends who love and support me and my work and demonstrate the best love and friendship has to offer. I also need to thank my agent Sally Apokedak for getting this book into the best shape possible and then getting it into the hands of my editor, Steve Geck, who further shaped it into the book it is today. I love you all!

About the Author

Jelly Bean Summer is Joyce Magnin's third book for young readers. Joyce grew up in Westbrook Park, Pennsylvania, which is near Philadelphia. She now lives on the other side of the country in Vancouver, Washington, with her very tiny dog named Minnie. Joyce enjoys books, video games, old movies, and cream soda.